### *"I want to se*

Natalie closed her eyes as her dress fell to the floor with a soft whoosh of fabric.

"Oh, God. Look at you.

She opened her mout
parted in a very flatter

She moved one foot b

"No, wait. Please. Leave those

She'd wanted new experiences. This definitely met the criteria.

"I know where I've seen you before," he said, his voice very low and rough. "On those pinup posters, with your ruby lips and your luscious curves."

She froze right there. Just stopped. Her? A pinup? With her plain white bra and panties?

He was the wrong Max, and yet...

There was no longer any need to pretend to feel sexy. Because she was truly feeling sexy. It was intoxicating. Freeing.

No one had ever looked at her that way, with his three undone buttons and his desire-darkened eyes, and she was going to revel in it.

He wanted a show.

So she would give him one....

Dear Reader,

It was so much fun writing *Choose Me, Have Me* and *Want Me,* the first three books in the It's Trading Men! miniseries. I got so many lovely letters and emails about the Hot Guys Trading Cards I had to write more!

In *Seduce Me,* Natalie Gellar, a film archivist in the East Village of New York, is looking for the right man. She wants to settle down, start a family. She's got her heart set on a librarian-friendly guy, someone who shares her values and her love of home. She can't believe her luck when she finds Max Zimm's Trading Card. He's not only a librarian, but he loves to cook and his passion is online gaming!

When Natalie finally sees Max's picture, she nearly passes out. Her nerdy, marriage-minded pick is literally a Hot Guy! He's tall, has gorgeous eyes and his smile could stop traffic. In person, he's even *hotter*.

Too bad the guy on the Trading Card is actually Max Dorset. Attorney. Playboy. One Night Stand.

I love to hear from readers! Visit my website, joleigh.com, and follow me on Twitter (@Jo_Leigh) and at tumblr.com/blog/joleighwrites/.

Look for the next book in the It's Trading Men! miniseries: *Dare Me*.

Happy Reading,

Jo Leigh

# Jo Leigh

## Seduce Me

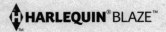
HARLEQUIN® BLAZE™

Recycling programs
for this product may
not exist in your area.

ISBN-13: 978-0-373-79800-1

SEDUCE ME

**Printed in U.S.A.**

www.Harlequin.com

## ABOUT THE AUTHOR

Jo Leigh is from Los Angeles and always thought she'd end up living in Manhattan. So how did she end up in Utah in a tiny town with a terrible internet connection being bossed around by a house full of rescued cats and dogs? What the heck, she says, predictability is boring. Jo has written more than forty-five novels for Harlequin. Visit her website at www.joleigh.com or contact her at joleigh@joleigh.com.

To get the inside scoop on Harlequin Blaze and its talented writers, be sure to check out www.blazeauthors.com.

### COSMO RED-HOT READS FROM HARLEQUIN
DEFINITELY NAUGHTY

All backlist available in ebook format.

To Birgit, who might love New York as much as I do,
and to Debbi Rawlins and Jill Shalvis, my intrepid
(and brilliant) plotting partners!

# _1_

"Okay, Ladies." Shannon Fitzgerald, the founder of the newest dating trend in Manhattan, had her arms up high, holding an open box. "Are you ready?"

No one answered. In fact, Natalie Gellar was pretty sure no one was even breathing. All twenty-four women in the room were leaning forward, though. Fingers at the ready, hope and anticipation doubling heart rates.

"On your mark…"

Five long utility tables had been pushed together into a rectangle on what was anything but a normal Wednesday evening in the St. Marks Church community room.

"Get set…"

Natalie stood her ground, shoulder to shoulder with the women around her, determined to do whatever was necessary to get the right card, the perfect card. The Hot Guys Trading Card that would change her life.

"Go!"

Shannon tossed the latest batch of cards into the center of the tables and sprinted out of the way.

As if they were attacking the first Black Friday sale table at Barney's, everyone went nuts.

Natalie grabbed whatever cards she could reach, skimming the writing, ignoring the pictures, tossing lawyers and accountants and musicians away like so much litter. Baseball fans, football fans, hockey fans. Ah, a reader, but crap, not the kinds of books she liked. Again and again, the cards were stirred. She heard squeals, disappointed moans, clapping and apologies as people wrestled for the same cards.

The word *librarian* made her heart skip a beat, and in the category of Marry, Date or One-Night Stand, his check mark next to Marry made her hands shake. Instead of listing a favorite restaurant, the card said he loved to cook and according to Tracy Jackson, the woman who'd submitted him, he was great at it. His passion was World of Warcraft, which wasn't her thing but she could totally deal with that. And then, oh, God, the bottom line: looking for a kindred spirit, someone who could be the Lilypad to his Marshmallow!

The reference to the sappy couple on *How I Met Your Mother* was the best gift ever. Not just because Natalie liked the show but because anyone who thought of himself in film or television terms was exactly the kind of man she was looking for. This was better than she'd hoped for. By a mile.

Now, to turn the card over. To see what Max Zimm looked like.

Her heart pounding after everything she'd read, she tried to calm down. After all, first impressions were as good as meaningless. Most everyone she found beautiful had started out as objectively nothing to write home about, but as she'd gotten to know them, they'd transformed. So even if Max had a handlebar mustache or googly eyes, she didn't care. At all. It was the inside that mattered, not the packaging.

After a deep breath, she turned the card over. And nearly fainted.

The nerdy librarian was a stunner.

"Who is that?"

Natalie tore her gaze from the picture of Max Zimm to look at her friend Denise. She'd introduced Natalie to the Trading Cards, bless her. "He's very good-looking, right?"

"*Very good-looking* doesn't quite cover it. Can I—"

"No."

Denise sighed. "Okay. But why did you pick him?"

Natalie turned the card over, hoping that she hadn't had some kind of neurological episode. "Librarian," she said. "Wants to get married. And he wants a Lilypad to go with his Marshall."

Her friend snatched the card out of Natalie's hand. "No. He. Did. Not. This is someone's idea of a joke. Oh, my God, who submitted him?" Denise continued to stare at Max Zimm's picture as she shouted, "Is Tracy Jackson here?"

Natalie gaped. Denise was the very picture of a demure librarian in her cardigan and cat-eye glasses, even though there was nothing else stereotypical about her. And now Natalie could add "bellows like a longshoreman" to the list of her friend's abilities.

No one responded, so Natalie turned her attention back where it belonged. "How could a librarian who looks like him live in Manhattan without us knowing about it?"

"I don't know." Denise shook her head. "Although we haven't met every one."

"But he'd be talked about. He'd go to conferences. We can't be that many degrees of separation from any librarian in this state. It doesn't make sense."

Denise lifted an arched eyebrow. "It does if he works for a think tank."

Natalie chewed on that for a moment. "Huh."

"He's probably some amazing genius who works for a top-secret government agency."

"S.H.I.E.L.D.," Natalie said. "He works for S.H.I.E.L.D."

"S.H.I.E.L.D. is fictitious," Denise said. "He's not one of the Avengers."

Plucking the card back from her drooling pal's hand, Natalie shrugged. "Then a S.H.I.E.L.D.-like agency. It could happen."

"Nat, he's already got the ability to stun with his looks. What else do you want?"

"Okay, true. Maybe he's new to the area. He could have been working anywhere. Europe, even."

"Who is that?" Iris Corcoran, a friend who was brand-new to Hot Guys Trading Cards, shouldered her way between Denise and Natalie. "And does he have a twin brother?"

Natalie just smiled and gripped the card more tightly.

"I thought you didn't care about looks," Iris said.

"It's not the front of the card that has me dazzled. It's the back."

Denise snorted.

"Fine, it's the front, too, but I would have chosen him anyway, no matter what he looked like."

"It sure doesn't hurt that he could be on the cover of *Gorgeous Guy Monthly,*" Iris quipped.

"He may look like a movie star, but don't let it go to your head. There are all kinds of guys here." Denise held up the card she'd picked. The man was pleasant-looking, slightly balding, with a very nice smile. "He plays the clarinet for the American Symphony Orches-tra."

"He's cute," Iris said. "Frankly, I'm just thrilled that

every single guy on a card has been personally submitted by someone in the group."

"I know, right?" For Natalie, the trading cards were truly a godsend, especially for a woman like her, who wasn't gorgeous, cared more about her work than her social life and tended to be a homebody. "Now that Oliver's out of the picture—"

"Oh, my God," Iris said, wincing. "I meant to call when I heard you guys broke up."

Natalie waved the wince away. "I'm fine about it. Better than fine. I had a feeling he was going to propose and instead of being happy, I was dreading it. When it finally happened, he didn't even bother with a ring. Said I should go pick one out myself. As long as it didn't cost more than forty-two hundred dollars. Talk about a major wake-up call. I don't know how I let it go on so long, really." She smiled at the too-good-to-be-true card she'd picked. "Max may be stunning, but if he's not the right man for me, I'll put the card straight back in the pile."

Iris squeezed Natalie's forearm. "Great attitude. One I intend to adopt as soon as I'm eligible. Don't get me wrong, I like that members have to submit men they know before they can select cards, but I can't wait! I already know three guys who want to be Hot Guys."

Denise leaned toward Natalie. "You decide to put that card back into the pot, I want to know about it first."

Just as she was going to respond, a woman she'd seen but not met leaned into their small huddle. "Someone asked about Tracy Jackson?"

"You're Tracy?" Denise asked.

"No, but she's a friend."

"She's not a practical joker, is she?"

"Tracy?" the woman asked as if the question itself

was nuts. "No. She's... No. She's really straightforward. She would have been here, but she's at a meeting in Toronto. She submitted two of her friends, though. I haven't met either one, but if Tracy likes them, they're bound to be top-notch."

Natalie relaxed. Not all the way. She would still call Tracy and get more information before she called Max. That would give her time to build up her courage.

"I'm Sandy, by the way. You're Denise, right? You work at the Columbia University library?"

Introductions were made, which was a good thing. It pulled Natalie back down to earth. Almost. She still couldn't get over Max's looks, but looks only went so far. He still needed to live up to the back of the card, which was no mean feat.

HE SHOULD GET UP, get showered, dressed, call someone, do something. According to the TV weather woman, anyone who wasn't outside frolicking under the clear blue sky was an idiot. It was day three of Max's three-week vacation, so he could do whatever the hell he wanted. After three years of operating on adrenaline, frolicking wasn't anywhere on his list. But he was hungry.

Max sighed as he gazed upon his best companion and constant source of succor: his 56-inch LED high-definition television. He couldn't remember what baseball teams were currently playing. After slipping in and out of sleep ever since he'd crawled onto the couch following a full nine hours in his bed, that wasn't a big surprise. Actually, he had no idea what the standings were, who was on the injury list, or if the Mets had any chance for glory. There'd been no fantasy baseball this year, or last year. Not for him, anyway. It was tragic. Some fan he was.

Again, he thought about going out. A simple proposition at face value, but, in fact, it would require him to make a series of decisions. What to wear, where to go, how to get there, whether to go alone? Try to hook up? He was exhausted just thinking about it. After such a long stretch of the hardest, most consuming work he'd ever faced, he didn't want to make another decision for the rest of his life. With one very big exception: what to do about his future.

It wasn't rhetorical. He really had to decide, and soon. Huh, he'd meant to call his dad again, get his advice this time instead of just saying a quick *hey,* but seeing as it was the middle of a workday, he figured he'd wait until that night to phone him.

The tort case had devoured his life, and that included not checking in regularly with his folks. They'd told him not to worry about it, but he missed them. And his brother. Mike was busy, too, with his newest art gallery. At least they texted from time to time.

Reaching behind him, Max adjusted his pillow and an unfortunate turn of his head made him realize he should have made the effort to shower several days ago. His sloth was all Manhattan's fault. The only exercise he'd gotten since he'd come home to rest was walking to the door to get his deliveries. Takeout, groceries, fluff-and-fold laundry. A person could get anything in this city, any day, any time. He loved the hell out of it.

What he also loved was burgers. His stomach gurgled and he snatched his cell phone from the coffee table. When he caught the actual time, his stomach made another loud protest and he hit speed dial fourteen. After ordering an Alpine Burger and fries from

Paul's Da Burger Joint, his hand dropped to his side like a dead weight. It wasn't possible to be this tired for so long. Maybe he was sick or something.

Or maybe he'd just worked hundred-hour weeks for three goddamned years with virtually no time off.

He grinned as he put his phone back on the table. It had been worth it. Every hour. Because right now the senior partners at Latham, Kirkland and Jones were deciding just how much money they were going to spend to make him happy. Happy enough to stay put. To ward off the headhunters, who'd already come calling. His firm had won an unwinnable case, due in large part to his ideas and hard work. The whole damn seafood industry was falling all over itself sending gift baskets and champagne to the office. Even better, they'd been congratulating him. Personally.

So, yeah. This break was not just going to rejuvenate him, it was going to make the firm sweat while Max considered every option available. Equity, naturally, but at what percentage? A new office? Use of the executive suite in London, absolutely, and the Malibu house in California.

Once he hauled himself off the couch, the shower appealed greatly. Stepping under the hot water relaxed his muscles and felt amazing. It even helped remind him that a real life was once again an option. At least until the next megacase.

Maybe later he'd venture out to his local watering hole. He liked Swift for its laid-back atmosphere, the good-looking women, excellent beer selection and… hell, the good-looking women were all that mattered.

By the time he finished shaving, his arms felt heavy

and his desire for action had diminished. The bar would be there tomorrow night. And maybe by then he'd be his old self again.

WITH TEN MINUTES to go until she had to leave St. Marks, Bobbie, a hairdresser Natalie had met at last month's meeting, pulled her aside to talk about the card Natalie had submitted. Randy was a friend of her tenant, Fred Mason. Both guys worked for the Museum of Modern Art and the three of them had bonded over their mutual love of cards and board games. Randy was a rock-solid, wonderful man. She'd actually entertained the idea of a romantic relationship with him, but he wasn't for her. He didn't care much for movies, which was a deal breaker.

After Natalie had offered a bunch of assurances about Randy, Bobbie whipped out her cell phone and called him. They had a date set up in under five minutes. Obviously thrilled, Bobbie looked at her card again, and then headed back to the other side of the room. Natalie didn't rejoin her friends, however. Not yet. She pulled out her Android. Toronto was in the same time zone, and it was only 7:00 p.m. Tracy Jackson might have time to talk.

"Hello?"

"Tracy, this is Natalie Geller from Trading Cards."

"Oh, hi. How's it going?"

Natalie cupped her free ear to block out the laughter and chatter in the room. "Great. I hope I'm not disturbing you."

"You're not, but I'm waiting for a car that's going to be here any minute. Did you pick one of my guys?"

"Max Zimm."

"Oh, he's wonderful. Exactly as advertised, I'm not

kidding. Really. You'll love him. Oops, my ride's here. Sorry."

"No problem. Go."

"Can you call again on Saturday? I'll be done with all this by then."

"Of course. Thank you." Natalie turned off the phone and looked at Max's face. His dark hair was a little on the messy side, but in that windblown, artfully tousled way that made her want to run her fingers through it. His lips hinted at a warm smile, and she had to admit, thick eyebrows completely worked on him.

What made her swallow hard, though, were his eyes. They were a fascinating mix of green close to the pupil and blue on the outer edges. Sectoral heterochromia. She'd never met a person with that genetic anomaly, but she'd grown up with a cat that had one brown eye and one green. She found it hard to look at the other parts of his face when those eyes were so unusually captivating. What must he look like in person?

Instead of reading his answers one more time, she kept on staring at his eyes, wondering what color he'd listed on his driver's license. He'd be like a chameleon, depending on what he was wearing.

At the thought of actually phoning him, anxiety shot through all her high hopes. Calling a man for a date was difficult enough, but picturing Max Zimm on the other end of the line made her want to hyperventilate. The men in her life had never been known for their eyes, or any other body part. Oliver was only memorable for not being memorable at all. He really should have been a spy or a thief, because he was so ordinary no one would think twice about him. He'd have gotten away with murder. But the only crime she knew he was capable of was leaving his thumb on the scale when he weighed corned beef for his customers.

Despite her nerves, Natalie would call Max. No, that wasn't quite accurate. She would call because of her nerves. So there.

# 2

ALTHOUGH HE HADN'T made it out the day before, by afternoon he hadn't been able to stand the confinement for one more minute. Max hurried out of his corner bodega, a man on a mission. He would drop off the groceries at his place and then catch a cab to the Upper East Side. He wanted Thai and he wanted it in a restaurant, and he wanted to get there by cab.

Four days of doing squat also turned out to be just enough time to drive home the fact that he hadn't had sex in months. A new and very uncomfortable record.

A survey of his contacts had showed him how tragically out of the loop he was. He'd started with Bev, his most reliable friend with benefits. She'd informed him that she was engaged and pointed out that if he'd ever once called her back or checked her Facebook or in any way remembered she was alive, he'd have known that.

The phone calls had gone downhill from there.

It disappointed him in a way that was new. He'd lost friends before. No one got to thirty and didn't, but he'd never let relationships die without meaning to. Some of these people he'd known since college. It was naive of him to think he could pick up right where he'd left off.

A cab pulled over and Max got in and gave the driver the address. After they merged into traffic, his cell phone rang, raising his hopes that one of his ex-friends had forgiven him. Then he saw the unfamiliar name on his caller ID. "Hello?"

"Max?"

"Yes."

"I'm Natalie. From the trading-card group."

Jesus. How had he forgotten the trading-card thing? His cousin Paula had pitched him the idea over a month ago, and he hadn't wasted a second signing on the dotted line. Thank God. "Right. Okay, hi, Natalie."

"You do know what I'm talking about, right?"

"Yes, of course."

"Good." She sounded nervous. "Because I picked your card."

"I'm flattered you chose me."

"Well, who wouldn't?"

Max laughed. "Lots of people."

"I can't imagine…" She cleared her throat. "I don't have much time because I'm in between appointments, but I thought I'd call you now because…well, because if I waited any longer I'd probably chicken out."

"You're doing great so far." Interesting that she'd told the truth. Equally interesting was the smile that had been on his face from the moment she introduced herself. Although that could be a result of having spent over an hour hearing that he was a persona non grata.

"A woman my age shouldn't have this much trouble asking for a date, though I'm new at this trading-card thing," she said, "but, anyway, I was thinking about dinner."

"Tonight?"

"No. Tomorrow night. If you want. Because tonight I have a class thing."

"Ah. Okay, tomorrow night would be great."

"Oh," she said, as if she'd expected him to object. "Where would you like to go?"

"Tell you what. You choose and I'll meet you there. Wherever you'd like, anywhere in the city."

"Seriously?" Her voice rose half an octave.

"Yes."

"What if I said Masa?"

He laughed. "That might be a problem." Max let that hang for a second before adding, "Getting a reservation there on a Friday night is difficult."

She chuckled, low and slightly breathy. "You're quick," she said. "I like it."

"I'm definitely intrigued. I'm also tempted to ask you some questions, but I think I'd rather wait until dinner. Keep the mystery going a little longer."

"Oh, good. No pressure at all."

"I hope not. It seems like an excellent way to meet. My expectation is to have a nice meal with pleasant conversation. If anything more happens, that's a bonus."

"I can work with that," she said. "How about seven o'clock at Lviv? That's in the Bowery, if that's all right?"

He'd heard of it, but never been. He lived near several eastern European restaurants, although they weren't very high on his list. "Sounds great. You'll have to find me, because I have no idea what you look like."

"And that doesn't make you nervous?"

"Nope. Excited."

"You're very brave."

"Only sometimes. Tell me, what really made you pick my card?"

She didn't say anything for a moment, and then it all came out in a rush. "I liked what you had to say. What you're looking for. But I really have to go now, so I'll see you tomorrow?"

"I look forward to it."

"Aside from being scared out of my wits, me, too," she said. Then she was gone.

Who was this woman? He could tell she was shy, which was appealingly uncommon for the girls he dated. He'd never actually been on a blind date, which this essentially was. Not once. He'd only lied a little bit when he told her his expectations. Especially given her last, rushed explanation for choosing him, he fully expected to end the evening back at her place. Hell, even if they didn't particularly click, it was only for one night. Whoever had thought up the trading-card idea deserved a Nobel Prize. Prevetted men with all their cards on the table, pun most definitely intended. Natalie would be the first of many, he assumed, a veritable feast of women who also wanted no-strings-attached one-night stands.

He settled back in the taxi, feeling a hell of a lot better than when he'd left his loft.

"What do you think?"

Fred gave Natalie a long, slow assessment from the ground up. "You can do better."

Her mouth dropped open as she stared at herself in her full-length mirror. "What's wrong with it?"

"Nothing's wrong. I just prefer your red dress."

"Why?" She knew it sounded as if she didn't trust him. He was never anything less than completely honest with her, even when a white lie wouldn't have hurt anyone.

"It makes your boobs look bigger."

Turning all the way to face him, she gave him her WTF stare. "This date isn't about my boobs. We're getting to know each other. That's all."

"It's always about boobs. Look, if you want better advice, I suggest you find someone who cares more about fashion. I have work to do. Aside from the boob issue, you look gorgeous. Like always. But if you want to make him swoon, go with the red dress and your black heels. And don't forget to put on the lip gloss, not just the lipstick." He shook his head. "We've been living in the same house too long. Why do I even know what lip gloss does for you? Where's Denise? I thought she was going to bring wine and you two were going to giggle and speculate until it was time for your date."

"She's at her cousin's bridal shower. In California. On vacation. And we don't giggle."

"I was being polite. Your friend sounds like an asthmatic horse when she laughs."

"She does not."

He sighed. "She doesn't in the same way that it's not about boobs." He stopped at Natalie's bedroom door. "Now have fun. If nothing else, at least you don't have to go to Oliver's mother's Shabbat dinner."

"She makes a great brisket."

He nodded. "That she does. But not good enough for you to stay with that schlub."

"Get out," she said, although she completely agreed with him. "I'm going to change into my red dress."

Fred, with his skinny black jeans, two-tone shoes and argyle sweater, walked down the hall. She didn't know anyone more fashion conscious than him. Damn hipster. If she didn't love him like a brother, he'd be impossible to put up with. The sound of the fridge door slamming told her the rat had stolen one of her expensive pale ales. He'd pay for that.

She pulled out her red dress even though she wanted badly to believe tonight's date wasn't about breasts. Yes, she wanted Max to think she was attractive and for the two of them to connect, but she didn't do casual hook-ups and she didn't like it when men assumed it was a done deal after a woman had spoken more than five words to them.

Pausing at her purse, she took out Max's trading card again. A man who played online role-playing games like World of Warcraft had to understand the value of patience.

THE BOWERY WAS close enough to Max's loft in NoHo to walk there easily. The clear, crisp May night invigorated him. As did the prospect of dinner and what might follow.

Not knowing Natalie's last name had removed the temptation of looking her up on Google. He liked that. There were far too few real surprises left in life. It was the age of spoilers—everything from movies to novels to credit scores were searchable. He liked to receive first impressions in person whenever possible. With a clean slate. Just hearing her voice had been enough to conjure images that were bound to be way off.

Lviv was down a flight of stairs. On the patio was a small grouping of outdoor tables, all occupied. It wasn't a jeans-and-T-shirts crowd, even though the weather was great, but not suits, either. Inside at the small bar, there was a big age range and a relaxed atmosphere. He assumed she'd chosen a place that was both familiar and comfortable, because she sure hadn't chosen it for a high-ticket meal.

He'd timed his entrance perfectly, but when a couple of minutes ticked by and no one approached, he turned back to the patio.

As he moved aside for a departing couple, he realized a lot of the people behind him at the bar weren't speaking English. It sounded Russian, but was probably, in this part of town, Ukrainian, which he understood was close.

The voices receded as his gaze caught on a great pair of legs coming down the stairs. The heels were black and high, almost stilettos, and one step later he got a glimpse of a red dress swinging against shapely knees. He waited in anticipation as the rest of her came into his line of sight.

She was curvier than a lot of women he knew, and he liked that. He didn't mind a thin body in his arms, although he preferred a softer experience. The red dress was tight around the middle, and the neckline showed off what appeared to be a hell of a nice rack. Dark hair bounced on her shoulders, soft curls that moved with her, and he only got a side view, but so far, he really hoped it was Natalie.

Dammit, now he'd done it. She'd probably walk into another man's arms and Natalie herself would disappoint him. Aw, hell. What was he thinking? There were a lot of beautiful women in the world, in this city, on this block. All different kinds. For all he knew, she could already be here, scoping him out.

Turning back to the bar, he didn't notice anyone craning to see the door. Behind him, a soft throat clearing made him smile.

It was the woman in red, and head-on she was… attractive. Not as stunning as some, but he wouldn't mind looking at her during dinner or across a mattress. "Natalie, I hope?"

She nodded. Held out her hand.

He shook it, glad for the few seconds' grace to adjust to the real woman. "Nice to meet you in person. I can't wait to learn more about you."

"I do have the advantage," she said, gripping her purse once she had her hand back.

"Not for long."

"Uh-oh. I guess fair is fair." She led the way to the hostess, who smiled brightly at Natalie and gave her a hug.

"I have a table ready. The best one," the hostess said, her accent strong. The woman pulled out a couple of menus, but before they moved, Natalie introduced them. The hostess was Mrs. Hanna Evanko—she owned the restaurant, along with her husband.

They were seated in a quiet corner where they wouldn't be bothered much. A simple round table with white linens. He held Natalie's chair, which earned him an approving nod from Mrs. Evanko before she slipped away.

He'd been given one of their large menus, but he put it aside for the moment. "Would you like wine with dinner?"

"I would," she said.

"Anything you recommend?"

"It's not a big selection, but everything is decent. My preference is red, although I'm flexible."

His brows rose, but only for a second. Certainly the double entendre was unintentional.

Natalie blushed like a nice rosé, confirming his supposition.

A younger woman wearing the simple black-and-white attire of the staff came to the table with a couple of candles. She looked as if she might be related to the owners. After she lit the candles, she looked at Max and said, "More romantic," in that same accent.

He caught the end of a sigh coming from Natalie. "Don't worry," she said. "They think being single is a disease. But they mean well."

"I have an aunt Ellen who's like that, although she's pretty much given up on me."

Natalie's eyes widened, but just for a second. Then she was looking at the menu. "Have you had much eastern European food?"

"No. I don't know why. What I have had, I've liked."

"If you have any questions, ask away."

"Am I the first trading-card guy you've gone out with?"

Startled, Natalie opened her mouth, but didn't speak right away. "Yes," she said, finally, but he got the feeling she wanted to say more.

He leaned forward, as if to tell her a secret, but he was actually checking out the dilation of her pupils, the way her breath caught on an inhale. "I'll make sure this evening lives up to your expectations." Then he sat back, picked up the menu he'd set aside and said, "Studenetz?"

Natalie blinked twice as she moved her gaze. She touched her lower lip with her index finger and looked at him again with a smile that might have been wicked if it hadn't vanished so quickly. "Fish in aspic."

"Ah. Sounds like that might be an acquired taste."

"You're right," she said, her voice reserved, almost formal. But that blush of hers hadn't disappeared yet. "I usually recommend the verenyky. Dumplings seem to be popular in every culture."

"I'll try those first."

She nodded. "Good. You can also try my borscht if you're daring."

"Oh, I'm daring, all right." This time he really was

talking about food, but watching her swallow gave him a clue where her mind had gone. Then the tip of her tongue swiped that same spot on her lower lip and he wanted to sample that instead.

"I see," she said. "Brave and daring. That's quite a combination, and we've just gotten started."

He shifted his gaze to his water glass, but a second later he was drawn back to her lips. He liked their shape. It was easy to imagine how they'd fit against his mouth. "Your turn," he said, just before he cleared his throat.

"To do what?"

"Tell me about yourself."

She glanced at him, then away. "The first thing you should know is that this isn't easy for me."

"What do you mean?"

After taking a deep breath, she met his gaze again and didn't waver. "The trading-card thing is an enormous stretch. I'm not what you'd call a social butterfly."

"What would you call yourself?" he asked, wishing the waitress had brought wine instead of a candle.

"I'm something of an introvert."

"Really?"

"It's not that I'm too shy to socialize or go places, but big crowds can be intimidating and sometimes I need time to recharge on my own. The reason we're at this restaurant is because I felt it would be easier to be around familiar people."

"That makes perfect sense. Including the part where this is a stretch for you…"

"You have no idea," she said, with a laugh. "So if it's all right with you, I'll start with the easiest question for me to answer. I'm passionate about film."

Max put his white napkin on his lap and watched her

do the same. "Film? I would have guessed books, but film is more intriguing."

"I do love books, but film caught my attention when I was young and never let go. Old ones. Black-and-white movies from the twenties, thirties and forties. Fritz Lang, Preston Sturges, Frank Capra, Michael Curtiz. I work at Omnibus. It's an art-film house and conservation center."

"I've been there."

She smiled, and it was as if he'd said the magic words that allowed her to relax completely. It was a good look on her. "Oh, nice. What did you see?"

"Um, it's been awhile. The last three years I haven't gotten out much. *Napoleon.* The Abel Gance silent film. I've been to a couple of short-film festivals, too, and a Buster Keaton retrospective."

"I was there. For all of those. I help run the programs."

"You're a fund-raiser?" He wanted more of this Natalie. She'd been smart to start out with something she cared about so deeply. The light in her eyes and the excitement in her voice were compelling. He could imagine her letting go, getting swept away in his arms. She wouldn't be quick about it, though, or easy. But she'd be worth the effort.

"That's only a part of what I do. I'm the librarian but also an archivist. I even teach film restoration and conduct tours of the facility. I'm a jill-of-all-trades, which means my schedule is insane, but I'm very happy. It's expensive to restore films, to keep the vaults at the right temperatures, buy the equipment. You should become a member."

He laughed at that. Couldn't help it. It made sense

that she helped with fund-raising. No one would be able to resist her.

"Sorry." Her cheeks blossomed with a flush that had a slightly different hue. Softer, somehow. "I crossed a line there. You don't have to buy anything."

"Don't worry about it. I can tell you're great at what you do. They're lucky to have you."

She fluttered her lashes, but it was more a sign of being flustered, he thought, than a flirtatious gesture. "Okay, now it's my turn, because I've been dying to know. How have we not met before? I thought I knew every librarian in New York."

"Excuse me?"

"My friend thought you might work at a think tank. Or maybe that you'd just transferred here."

Max wasn't sure what was going on. "I work at a law firm."

"Oh. Okay. I imagine big firms have large libraries."

"Natalie, I'm not a librarian. I'm a lawyer."

"Wait. What? You're...not—" She put her purse on the table and pulled out his card. He only got a glimpse, but that was definitely his picture. "—Max Zimm?"

He slowly shook his head, feeling as confused as she looked. "Max Dorset."

"Oh," she said, and sank back in her chair. "But..." She studied the card and when she looked at him again she was clearly mortified. She'd tensed like a watch spring and averted her gaze. "I don't understand."

"Neither do I. I mean, obviously that's my picture, but not my name."

"I—I don't even know what to say. Except I'm so sorry."

"It's not your fault," he said, some of the confusion beginning to lift. "Clearly someone at the printing company messed up. What else does the back of the card say?"

Her lips parted with a distressed gasp. "This whole trading-card thing. I never should've—" She shook her head and cleared her throat. "Look, it's still early." She calmly put her napkin on the table and stood. "I hope you can salvage the rest of the evening. I really do. I'm sorry to have wasted your time."

Before he could even make sense of what was going on, Natalie was halfway across the room.

# 3

SHE SHOULD HAVE known he was too good to be true. Stupid, stupid. So much for her brave new life. If she had any brains at all, she'd go running back to Oliver. He might be dull as dishwater but he was steady and she'd never have to worry about competition for him.

Hanna called out to her, but Natalie kept going, darting around acquaintances she didn't want to see, damning her high heels. She should take them off, run away as quickly as possible.

"Natalie, wait."

God, it was Max. Max Dorset. An attorney so out of her reach it made her blush to her toes. Why hadn't she said his last name when she'd called him? That would have saved them both this humiliation.

She'd made it through the patio to the base of the stairs when his hand on her arm stopped her.

"Wait, please," he said. "Please."

She couldn't simply shake him off. None of this was his fault. But facing him felt like torture. "I should be getting home," she said. "I can't say how very sorry I am for the mix-up."

"I don't blame you."

"Still, I can't imagine that you were looking for someone like me when you filled out your trading card."

"How do you know?"

She met his gaze finally and instead of seeing mockery in his green-blue eyes, she recognized honest confusion. "You don't play World of Warcraft, for one."

"You're right," he said. "But I have played a hell of a lot of Legend of Zelda and Mortal Kombat."

"Recently?"

"No."

His gentle smile made it possible for her to take a deep breath without bursting into flames. "Something tells me you also aren't looking to get married."

"Not at the moment, no. But I was looking for a nice time with a fascinating woman, and I got that. What I don't understand is why it needs to end so quickly."

Natalie couldn't speak for a second. She hadn't been prepared for this, and she wasn't sure if his being great about the mistake wasn't the best reason of all for her to walk away and not look back. "We both know I'm not your kind of woman, but thank you for being so nice about it."

"I'm not sure I have a type," he said, and despite his smile, she didn't believe that. "If I wasn't enjoying myself, I would have made an excuse to take off like a shot. Now, why don't we go back inside? I'd still like to hear the rest of your answers. And find out what you found so appealing about this Max Zimm."

Out of the corner of her eye, Natalie saw a white shirt, a white chef's hat and a very large, angry man walking with purpose. Behind him, half the staff followed.

"Oh, crap. I probably should have mentioned that Hanna is my aunt." She spoke quickly, intending to head off the disaster. "In fact, everyone who works here is related to me in some way."

"Why, 'oh, crap'?" he asked, turning to look. His body stiffened and for a second she thought he was going to bolt.

"Uncle Victor," she said, stepping out in front of Max. "Stop, please." Holding out her hands slowed the oncoming horde. "He hasn't done anything wrong. Max has been a complete gentleman. We've just had a misunderstanding."

The army stopped advancing, although Uncle Victor didn't look very mollified. "What kind misunderstanding?"

"There was a mix-up. I thought he was someone else and I was embarrassed. So if you could all go back inside, that would be good."

Five pairs of eyes, not including Natalie's, stared at Max as if they wanted him to swear a blood oath that every word she'd said was true. To his credit, his smile almost seemed real.

"Go on," she said, herding them back. "Someone's probably stealing all the spoons. I'll report in later."

"You come back in," Hanna said. "Victor will cook something special, okay?"

"No, thank you, Titka. I don't want to go back now. I'll call you tomorrow."

*"Vī pevni?"* Hanna asked.

Natalie widened her smile. "Yes, I'm sure."

Her aunt leaned closer, and in a whisper that could have been heard in Times Square, said, "He's very handsome."

"I know he is, but someone's waiting to pay for their meal," Natalie said, then watched until the whole lot of them were inside.

Max cleared his throat. "I suggest we get the hell out of here before they change their minds."

"Excellent idea."

Halfway up the stairs, he touched her arm again. It was sweet. He was being sweet. It made her nervous and a little more excited than was wise.

Once on the street, he tugged her near the store behind them. "I don't know about you," he said, "but I'm hungry enough to eat my shoe. Let's try this again. Start fresh. Eat. Have a drink. Talk?"

She should say no. It was utterly unlike her to even consider doing otherwise.

"Come on. We've already been through maximum discomfort, right?"

She didn't argue, although she could think of half a dozen ways things could get worse. However, Max being such a mensch had her renewing her vow to never, ever go back to Oliver. Which meant getting back on the horse. No more running away like a child. "All right. But only under two conditions."

His eyes narrowed and, damn, suspicion looked good on him. "What would those be?"

"You pick the restaurant. And when we talk, we don't mention the cards at all."

"Deal," he said, his grin crooked and fine. "I know just the place." Taking her hand in his, he walked her to the curb and hailed a taxi. He held the door for her, then gave the cabbie an address in the West Village.

THE LAST PIECE of pizza margherita was tempting, but Max let it go. He didn't want to be too full, not for the night he had planned. Coming to Trattoria Spaghetto had been just the thing. It was an old-school restaurant—good food and decent house wine that had been served quickly.

"I still don't know what kind of law you practice,"

she said. "All we've talked about is movies." She dotted her lips with her napkin and sipped her Chianti.

She'd been right to ban the mention of the cards. Not that he didn't want to know things about her, aside from what she looked like out of that dress. The conversation had been easy once they'd settled in, and Natalie really was interesting. She could write a book about old films and restoration, a topic he'd never considered worth his time, but he'd read it cover to cover. Now that it was his turn to talk about work, he didn't want to. Surprising, since he'd been basking in the praise from his victorious precedent-setting case.

"I've liked discussing movies," he said. "It's a lot more interesting than tort law."

"I don't know much about that. I mean, I know that tort is civil law, like personal injury or class-action suits, but I have no idea what you actually do."

"Infrequently, I'm in court, which can be interesting and tense, although compared to trials in films, real court is long and plodding. It's a great remedy for insomnia."

"More frequently?"

"It's a lot like having homework every day of your life. Looking up precedents, and not just recent ones. One time I actually used something from the ancient Greeks to help hone a point."

"Huh," she said. "That's what librarians do."

"Yeah, but they don't get to bill for the hours."

"And more's the pity." She pushed her hair back over her shoulder, turning her head to look at the neighboring table.

He took the opportunity to look down at the soft roundness of her breasts, the contrast between the scarlet of the dress and her pale skin. For the last forty minutes, he'd hardly looked away from her eyes. They were brown, not a particularly memorable shade, but with their passion and subtle drama they'd held him captive.

Jesus, the longer he was with her, the more he wanted her. Although he couldn't help wondering if this level of attraction would have been there if he hadn't been living like a monk for such a long time.

"I'm full," she said, facing him again. "And glad we did this."

"You're not throwing in the towel yet, are you? It's still early."

"Maybe for you. But I'm very dull. By ten most nights I'm already in my PJs watching TV."

"There's nothing good on, trust me. But it is a great night out. What do you say we go for a walk?"

"In these heels?"

"Oh, right."

"You look so disappointed," she said, her delight clear in her voice.

"I am. I was looking forward to talking some more."

"I suppose we could go for a few blocks. I'll cry uncle when it's too much."

"You could just take them off."

"Barefoot in Manhattan? I'm not sure if I'm caught up on my tetanus shots."

He leaned across the small table and put his hand on hers. Her eyes widened as she stared, then a faint blush tinted her cheeks. "We don't have to walk far to get to my place. I've got some Courvoisier, which goes great with a to-go order of the Italian cheesecake."

Natalie's blush deepened. "I don't think that's a very good idea."

"Why not?"

"I don't really do things like that," she said, pulling her hand out of his grasp.

"What, eat cheesecake?"

Pressing her lips together for a moment, her gaze swept over his face, everywhere except his eyes. "Cognac and cheesecake at your place? Perhaps to see your etchings?"

He didn't respond immediately, knowing she'd eventually meet his eyes. When he got the look he wanted, he lowered his voice. "I don't think guys use etchings anymore, but if I did, would that be so bad?"

Natalie cleared her throat, turned her wineglass forty-five degrees and gave him a hesitant smile. "It would be flattering. Also a waste of time."

She sounded very sure and serious, and he wasn't the kind to hear yes when a woman said no. But everything about her body language read that she wasn't quite as certain as she'd like him to believe. Still, he nodded. "I know we decided not to talk about the cards, but I'm curious. You clearly do want to settle down. Get married. You seem young. Or maybe it's just that the women in my field tend to be in their thirties before they start to think about marriage and kids. The career track in large firms is brutal."

"I'm not that young," she said. "Twenty-seven seems a good age, especially because I want children someday."

He nodded. "Makes sense."

She tapped the edge of her glass with her index finger. "I'm also terrible at dating."

"I beg to differ."

She dismissed his comment with a wave. "You don't count. You did when I thought we shared the same goals, but once that was cleared up…"

"I think I feel insulted."

"Why? You're allowed to not want what I want. And anyway, I tried to bow out, give you a chance to go find someone more your speed, but you blew it."

"I think I chose wisely. You make me want to see old movies with you. No wonder they have you giving tours at Omnibus. Your passion is very engaging."

She studied him with a tentative frown, as if she was trying to decide whether to believe him. "Thank you," she said finally.

"Now, how about that dessert? Coffee?"

Natalie shook her head, causing her dark hair to tumble over that obstinate shoulder. "As great as the cheesecake sounds, I'm going to say no."

He shook his head. "That's a shame. I've got a terrible sweet tooth. Which means I have to spend far too long at the gym, because I'm not that great at denying myself."

"Well, that's one thing we have in common. Not the gym part." She shuddered. "I walk, of course, and I go to yoga twice a week. But big machines and weights? Not for me."

"Whatever you're doing works," he said, and even though it was probably a nonstarter, he didn't hold back on his smile.

"You must be a very good lawyer," she said.

"You think?"

"You're very smooth."

"Huh. I could take that one of two ways."

Natalie flashed that wicked smile he'd seen earlier. "I'll amend that to convincing."

"Better." He smiled back. "That's because I'm telling the truth."

"Thank you," she said, giving him a small bow.

He couldn't help it. He reached out for her hand again, not sure if she'd put it within reach consciously or not. "Is it at all possible that there's room in your plan for something a little less permanent until Mr. Right comes along?"

When her teeth scraped against her full bottom lip, he felt his cock stir. It wasn't the first time that had happened since they'd met, but it was the most insistent. But he doubted words would work when actions said so much more. He leaned in farther, not hiding his desire at all as he gently teased the tender skin of her inner wrist.

NATALIE WAS EQUAL parts suspicious and tempted. The way he looked at her with such hunger was like something from a movie. However, that, along with his very gentle touch, meant it was also possible that she was being played. In fact, that was likely the case. The question was, did she mind?

There was a reason she didn't do one-night stands. His name was Cory and she'd met him in college. She'd been won over by his love of literature and the way he'd looked at her. They'd clicked on a level that had been entirely new. The night had been magic. They'd made plans. He never called her again. When she'd run into him at a book signing, he'd said *hey* in a way that made it clear he couldn't remember her name.

After that, she had a boyfriend for the last two years of undergraduate studies; another, Tim, for almost all of grad school; and Oliver. Max was another creature altogether. He was gorgeous, sexy, smart. A sophisticated man who belonged to Manhattan in a way she never would. She was a child of her neighborhood. He was skyscrapers and after-hours clubs. She'd only crossed paths with the likes of him at work.

Was she up for something that risky? Although, was there a risk at all, if she walked in with no expectations? Frankly, it would have been easier to throw caution to the wind if she'd worn matching underwear.

His thumb on her wrist was right over her pulse. No way he could miss how her heart was beating *allegrissimo*. But then, the way he looked at her made her feel entirely exposed, as if he could read every thought.

She wished he would say something. Blink. Because if he didn't, she was going to say yes. The hell with her blue polka-dot panties and her plain white bra.

He didn't say a word, but his gaze was a blatant promise of things she'd only read about.

"How far did you say your place was?"

## 4

NATALIE'S FIRST IMPRESSION of Max's loft was that she
didn't belong in it. Nothing was overstuffed or sec-
ondhand. Of the few things he had, a lot were shiny
and black and his television was bigger than her stove.
Her second impression was that the only way she'd get
through the next part of the evening was if she considered this a visit to another country. She'd always been
a brave traveler, never afraid to try the local cuisine or
explore the dodgy side of the tracks.

"Courvoisier?" he asked, putting the box of cheesecake on the glossy counter that divided the kitchen from
the minimally furnished living room.

"Please." Noting the bare-but-for-an-elaborate-coffee-
maker countertop, she doubted he did much cooking. The
well-stocked wet bar looked as if it got a lot more use.

He brought down two snifters from the top shelf
and poured them each a generous finger of the cognac.

"My parents liked Rémy Martin," she said. "My father was a cellist for the New York Philharmonic and
he received a bottle every Christmas from the concert-
master. That was the only time they used their snifters.
When I was a girl, I used to sneak Coke in them. I imagined myself being terribly sophisticated as I swirled my

soda, then sipped elegantly even though the carbonation never stood a chance against the heat from my palms."

He gave her a glass and a smile. "Who were you terribly sophisticated with?"

"Movie stars, mostly. From black-and-white films, of course. Cary Grant was my favorite."

"Okay, there's no way I can compete with Cary Grant." Max watched her swirl her drink as he did the same. "My folks didn't do a lot of drinking, but when they did, it was beer. They had a few bottles of hard liquor for guests, but that's it."

She looked over his collection of liquor. "You ended up with excellent taste."

"Don't tell anyone, but I took a class. Okay. More than one. The year between NYU and law school, I learned about wine. That was interesting, and I liked the tasting part, so I took another class that included hard liquor."

"Very practical," she said. "I imagine the knowledge has been especially useful in your line of work."

"If you count sounding like a pretentious ass useful."

She grinned. "I doubt you made a single mistake."

Stepping closer to her, he lifted his glass. "I'm glad you're here."

"Me, too." She clinked her glass against his and lifted the snifter to her lips, figuring it was safe enough to take a sip now that some of the alcohol had evaporated. Not only was she wrong, but her sip went down the wrong way and sent her into a fit of coughing that doubled her over.

Thankfully, Max didn't pat her on the back. He just disappeared for a bit, and then took her cognac, replacing it with a glass of water.

Finally, after a ridiculously long and painful time, the

spasms stopped and she was able to breathe again. Naturally, she'd teared up and could only imagine the mascara damage. "Bathroom?" she croaked as she grabbed her purse from the counter.

"Come on." He touched her arm again, in that same spot behind her elbow. "I'll show you."

She closed the bathroom door and leaned her head against it, afraid to look in the mirror. What the hell had she been thinking? Coming to his place had been a disaster waiting to happen, and they hadn't even gotten to the naked part yet.

For a minute there, it had felt right. More like her teenage dreams than her adult reality. But she'd maxed out her courage simply by meeting him at the restaurant, let alone coming here. To imagine doing more was absurd.

It might be the chance of a lifetime, but if she died of stress in the middle of sex that would probably be a net loss.

Pushing off from the door she braved the mirror. The bathroom was very cool and modern, like the rest of the loft. Tiny, of course, with just a toilet and sink. He must have an en suite by the bedroom.

Well, she wouldn't be finding out anytime soon. A tissue and some careful dabbing got rid of the mascara tracks. She added a fortifying coat of her Chanel Velvet Rouge but didn't see the point of adding lip gloss. Then she practiced her exit line in the mirror, the way she always practiced giving speeches. Nothing clichéd because he'd been so nice, and she'd come willingly. Besides, she could afford to admit the truth. They'd never see each other again.

*They'd never see each other again.*

Her red-rimmed eyes widened as she thought about

that. Even after the coughing debacle, she knew he wasn't going to kick her out the door. He liked her. They'd connected in their odd way, and she was glad she'd met him. The one thing that might cause her regret, shockingly, would be quitting now.

Clearly, Max Dorset had some smooth moves, which undoubtedly came from plenty of experience. He was an amazing man, and she imagined he could walk into any bar or club in town and find himself with a wealth of opportunities.

One thing Natalie knew for sure was that the best way to learn anything was to find a teacher who was deeply passionate about the subject. Not that she knew for a fact that Max was a sex aficionado, but it was more than an educated guess. What might she learn from him?

The woman in the mirror blushed, but so what? They'd never see each other again. It would mean getting naked, which would really give her something to blush about. If she let him see the travesty of her underwear. If not, that meant turning out the lights, which would be comforting in one way, but dammit, when would she ever be in bed with someone that handsome again? If she was going to do this thing, she wanted to see what was going on.

So, she'd make a joke about her panties. God, they were full briefs. Polka-dot full briefs. There were no jokes funny enough.

With a sigh, she turned to leave, but stopped before her hand hit the doorknob. She could take them off now. Put them in her purse. He'd think she hadn't worn any, which was not a terrible option.

Lifting her dress was simple enough, but actually removing her underwear was daunting. She really intended to do this thing. To have sex with a man she barely knew with no expectations of anything else. Not a follow-up phone call, no second date. And no expectations meant she wouldn't be crushed by disappointment when neither of those things happened.

The polka dots hit the floor. Color rose to her cheeks. Again. But so did a grin. No use walking into this unless she was prepared to have a great time. Which she most certainly was.

"Take that, Oliver, you big idiot," she said, straightening her back and running her hands down her body, surprised at how naughty it felt to be bare down below. "All this could have been yours. Ha."

With that, and at the last second remembering to fold up her panties and stuff them in her purse, she opened the bathroom door.

Max stood a few feet in front of her in his white poplin shirt, the sleeves rolled, baring strongly corded forearms. When her gaze moved back to his face, his tentative grin broadened. Before she took her third step, he was inches away. She had to look up to meet his eyes. His finger brushed her cheek, light as a feather.

"Eyelash," he said, even though she knew it was a lie.

Her lips parted, but whatever she'd been going to say slipped away when he leaned in for a cognac-flavored kiss. It was mesmerizing. Surprisingly intimate.

A second passed, then another. They moved together at the same time. Slow, in stages. Lips against lips, the tip of his tongue tracing the seam in between hers until she let him in. She made a sound that wasn't quite a whimper, and it must have been the sign he'd been waiting for.

He brought their bodies together as the kiss deepened. All she could think was that this wasn't her life.

No man had ever felt this way before, had ever been as smooth or sure. And, thank God, she'd never see him again. Coming this far had been brave. Going further was a crazy risk.

But this was the new Natalie, and she wanted— needed—to know how much she would dare.

MAX RAN HIS hands down Natalie's back, stopping just under her waistline. He'd take his time with her. That she was in his arms was his great luck, but he could tell she wasn't entirely certain she should be. Now that he'd felt her against him, how she curved in the middle, he wasn't about to lose her to his own impatience. It wasn't exactly a hardship to move back up again, to feel her twitch under her sexy red dress. Not when her nipples were so hard.

He was getting hard himself, and shifted his hips so his nascent erection wouldn't spook her.

She huffed against his lips, and then shocked the hell out of him with a firm hand on his right butt cheek, which got his attention.

"You don't have to tiptoe," she whispered, her mouth barely an inch away from his own. "I'm not a virgin or a delicate flower."

It was a good speech, and he would have bought it completely if she hadn't been trembling. "I can see that," he said, holding himself very still. "But I don't want you to regret this."

She breathed out and he inhaled. "I've got you for one night, and then we'll never see each other again," she said. "I doubt I'll have another opportunity like it. Please don't think I'm exploiting you for your sexuality." Her brow furrowed, then relaxed. "Scratch that. I do want to exploit you for your sexuality. If you have no objections."

"Can't think of one. Please, be my guest. Anything you'd like."

"Anything?"

"Within reason."

She pulled back to look at him. Her cheeks were pink, her pupils had taken over her beautiful brown eyes and her lips looked swollen and well kissed. Perfect. "'Within reason' covers a lot of territory."

He grinned. "No lasting scars. At least, not where they'd show."

Her laugh was as sexy as her chutzpah. "I have no intention of hurting you. But you should know I haven't had a great deal of experience. With men."

"I understand. I'll do my best to expand your horizons."

"I don't need acrobatics or accessories. Just, well, I hope like crazy that the men I've been with were… unskilled. Because there hasn't been one single bell or whistle."

Now he leaned back. "You've never had an orgasm?"

Her eye roll was impressive. "Of course I've had an orgasm." Then she hid those same wicked eyes with her lowering lashes. "I've never been given one, though."

"Ah. Okay," he said, the word stretching as he thought of everything that could go wrong. "I'll do my best."

"I don't mean to pressure you or anything."

He had to laugh. "Tell you what. Let's both just have a good time."

"Yes. Yes, that's what I want." She nodded. "Although you're probably limp as a noodle by now."

"You don't have an internal censor at all, do you?"

She removed her grip from his ass. "Too much, right?

When I'm nervous I either clam up completely or say everything that comes to mind. But I can tone it down. I'm sorry. I got carried away."

"No," he said, putting her hand back where it'd been. "I don't mind, I swear. In fact, I like it. Keep on saying what you want. If I do something that doesn't sit right, tell me."

"Deal," she said. "But how do we get back to before?"

He pulled her close, proving that the talk had done nothing to diminish his enthusiasm. "All you have to do is be yourself and I'll be fine."

Natalie met his gaze for several long seconds before she kissed him. Holy crap, did she ever.

LETTING GO OF every kiss she'd had in the past wasn't difficult. It was a relief. Secretly, Natalie had always suspected she could be one of the great kissers of all time, but she'd never been with anyone who truly inspired her.

Max made her bold. Committing herself to…this… was as intoxicating as champagne, as the moment when Fred Astaire sees Audrey Hepburn running down the steps at the Louvre like Winged Victory herself. With Max, she could be as silly or foolish or dramatic as she liked, and not obsess over her embarrassment for the rest of her life. Because she wasn't going to be embarrassed. Nor was she going to see him again. It all worked out.

Although she still did have to take off the rest of her clothes. The hell with it. Tonight, she had the body of a goddess and the courage of Katniss Everdeen.

His hands ran down her back as he mapped out the territory. Did he realize she had gone commando? It seemed so, from his surprised grunt and the press of his erection against her tummy. Things were in motion. And wouldn't that just shock every person who'd ever met her.

She decided to do some exploring of her own, even as they kissed as if it was going out of style. To her delight, he knew just how much to open his mouth, how to not try to swallow her face. That he tasted like expensive cognac was a liqueur-soaked cherry on top.

But the real treat was having free rein over his unbelievably fine body. She didn't give one solitary damn that her thoughts were as shallow as a wading pool. His muscles rippled. Rippled. How many times had she read that, imagined that? Despite the thrilling sensation of Max lightly sucking on her lower lip, she giggled.

In another one of his smooth moves, he let her lip go and asked, "What's so amusing?" then picked up directly where he'd left off.

"Amazing," she said, although the word was so hopelessly garbled, she didn't even try to go on. Talking was not her priority at the moment. In fact, touching him through his clothes seemed a waste. Like nibbling on crackers when a whole banquet was on offer.

Without too much effort, she was able to sneak her hands between their chests. Undoing his buttons was a little more difficult than she'd imagined. Mostly because she was so greedy, wanting every sensation at once.

But Max let her know he was on the same page by finding her zipper with no trouble at all. He lowered it expertly, then put his hands on her bare back, just below her bra strap.

It shouldn't have felt so different. Oliver had touched her there plenty of times. But she'd never once shivered from top to toe, wiggled her shoulders and her hips, or whimpered.

He groaned in response and she remembered about the buttons, continuing down the line. When he undid her stupid white bra with a single, elegant flick, she might have lost it for a minute. Hands flat on his shirt, she found her forehead resting on his shoulder.

He kept rubbing down the naked part of her back. "You okay?"

"Umm."

"Is that a yes?"

She nodded enough for him to feel it. "You're very good at this," she said, just before taking a deep breath and looking at him once more.

He only smiled and slid his hands underneath her bra to cup both her breasts. "You feel good." Dipping his head, he kissed behind her ear. "But I really want to see you," he murmured against her skin.

"Oh." Her eyes had drifted closed and she couldn't seem to lift her lids. "Okay."

In seconds he'd led her to his room, to his very large bed. The spread was burgundy, the wood of the frame dark, maybe cherry or teak. It was a guy's room, with heavy pieces and neutral tones, but the framed oil painting above the bed was an abstract with vivid reds and yellows and turquoise. Very surprising.

He cleared his throat and she quickly forgot about the decor. It was showtime. The bedside lamp was turned on, and she had to decide if she was going to say something about that, or let it be.

Turning it off really would make her feel more comfortable.

Katniss wouldn't turn off the lights.

Natalie wouldn't, either.

He must have seen her determination, or maybe he just didn't want to wait anymore. Before she'd even registered the move, her sleeves were sliding down her arms, along with her bra straps. Looking down, she was startled to find her breasts naked, her nipples hard and very there as her dress pooled at her waist, caught by her belt.

Max moaned as he cupped her breasts. "You're gorgeous," he murmured. "I want to look at you. All of you." He tackled her belt, which wasn't much of a challenge, and she closed her eyes as her dress fell to the floor with a soft whoosh of fabric.

"Oh, Christ. Look at you. I never expected—"

She opened her eyes to find him staring, his lips parted in a very flattering way.

He stepped back until he was no longer touching her, then one more step so he could sit on the edge of his bed, as if looking at her made him lose his sense of balance.

She moved one foot back to take off her heels, and jumped at his, "No, wait. Please. Leave those on."

He didn't look as though he was kidding. Especially when he pressed his palm against his very obvious hard-on.

She'd wanted new experiences. This definitely met the criteria. She curled her right shoulder and knee, although it didn't hide very much. Not that hiding was exactly what she wanted to do, but being stared at like that was kind of intimidating.

"Oh, I know where I've seen you before," he said, his voice very low and rough. "On those World War II pinup posters, with your ruby lips and your luscious curves."

She froze right there. Just stopped. Her? A pinup? She loved those women, those images, had one framed in her office. It was probably the dress that had done it. Or her hair. It was what she'd always wanted people to see, but they never did. Never had.

He was the wrong Max, and yet...

There was no longer any need to pretend to feel sexy. Because she was. Truly. Like Betty Grable or Marilyn Monroe. It was intoxicating. Freeing.

No one had ever looked at her that way, with his three undone buttons and his desire-darkened eyes, and she was going to revel in it.

He wanted a show, and she gave him one. Slow and naughty, with a soundtrack in her head and a sharp need to press her thighs together.

This night had been fantastic. Even if he didn't give her an orgasm it was already the best ever. She owed a great big thank-you to whoever had messed up the trading card, because tonight, she was her own dream come true.

# 5

Max finished the job she'd started on his buttons and threw his shirt somewhere. He wanted to stand up, but what if she stopped? Watching her do her little hootchy-kootchy number was one of the greatest things he'd ever seen. She was awkward and sexy and embarrassed and brave, but she was also naked except for her red lips and her black heels, and he wanted her like fire.

Her breasts were great. Real and great and he already knew they were so soft he'd like to just hold on to them for about a week. Then there was her hourglass shape. If he'd ever gone out with a woman with a figure like hers, he'd have remembered that. Her hair, her lips, her slightly pooched tummy, the trim vee of her pubes—everything seemed so innocent it was terrible how much he wanted to spread her out like a picnic.

He stood, unable to sit still any longer, and sure enough, she stopped. Put her hand over her face. It killed him. He touched her shoulder, then her hair. "That was beautiful," he said, slowly putting his arms around her. "Thank you."

"I've never done that before."

"I'm so glad you did." He kissed her, holding back, taking his time. It was important for her to relax. At least the trembling from before was gone. When she parted her lips and swiped his upper lip, he figured they were doing just fine.

She might not be a delicate flower, but she definitely was more than ordinary. In school, at work, just living in Manhattan, he'd never come across someone quite like her.

He was glad she knew the score, though. A woman like Natalie needed more attention than he could give. One night, sure. In fact, one night would be perfect.

"Let's—" He led her the few steps to his bed and folded down the covers. Natalie sat, and he could tell by the way she curled her shoulders he needed to do something now so she wouldn't feel so self-conscious.

Undoing his pants got her attention. He had nothing to be worried about in the junk department, but she really needed to blink soon or he was going to get a complex. Her staring so hard was kind of sexy, but then, what wasn't when it came to tonight? Besides, he'd practically popped a vein when her dress had dropped. She couldn't have surprised him more. Well, maybe if she'd told him back at the restaurant that she wasn't wearing panties.

The only thing he could do was finish getting naked as efficiently as possible, because if he kept thinking about that, he was going to pop before he made her come. When he straightened up, her lips had parted and her eyes were as dark as midnight. His cock twitched so hard it bounced against his stomach.

She jerked back in surprise.

No longer able to stand being so far from her, he helped her scoot over to the middle of the bed so her head was on the pillow and her bare feet touched the edge of the folded linens.

What a sight she was. Her hands slipped down to

cover her breasts, and then moved down, revealing her hard, deep pink nipples. He had no real clue what made her embarrassed and what didn't, but one thing he knew for sure: what happened next needed to be perfect. For her. A grand slam. All the bells and every whistle.

Once he was finally next to her, he cupped her face with his hands. Holding her steady, he kissed her deeply, and he couldn't have stopped if the ceiling caved in.

Touching her from chest to knee, it was all he could do not to spread her legs and thrust into her and keep going until he passed out. But he curbed his impulse, choosing instead to smooth his hands from her breast to her belly, caressing the curve of her waist, her hips, her sides, and then lower still.

The tips of his fingers stroked gently along the vulnerable skin of her inner thighs. "You comfy?" he asked.

"Yes," she said, drawing out the word into a long hiss of satisfaction as he brushed the soft hair of her pussy. Patiently, while he stole kiss after kiss, he stroked her open.

She sighed with pleasure, but he wanted more.

"Tell me." He dipped the pad of his middle finger into her, sliding the wetness up to her clitoris, tracing swirls around and around the hard bud, relishing the feel of it as it hardened under his touch. Her breathing changed, became shallower, her kiss wetter. "Remember, you can ask for anything you want."

"I like you touching me," she whispered.

When she kissed him again, it went on for a long slow time when she explored the soft slick on the back side of his upper lip, then back down, testing, teasing. His finger never stopped moving inside her warmth, growing bolder as the tension built. She jerked her hips, a little spasm, a preview.

He kissed her chin and nipped down her neck, breathing in her hot scent as he continued to make her writhe. He wanted to taste her, but not this time. Not yet. Now he wanted to watch her come apart.

She moaned as her body started trembling again, a whole different kind of quiver. Hips thrusting, breasts rising and falling with each deep breath. He looked down to find one hand gripping the sheet, the other moving on her belly, her middle finger mimicking the quick flicker he used on her clit. Damn.

She shifted on another moan. He pressed his mouth to the tender skin just below her ear, while one finger, then two glided into her.

Her body stiffened further and he leaned back so he could see her, careful to keep his thumb rubbing her clitoris even as his fingers plunged into her wet heat.

"Oh, God," she said, her voice as tight as her body. "Oh—"

She spasmed around him, arching off the mattress, squeezing his fingers. Her hand pulled the sheet until he thought it might tear. He didn't stop as she moaned words he couldn't make out, as she gasped and twitched.

He was harder than he'd been in a hell of a long time. One brush of his cock against her skin would set him off. Watching her climax was so damn hot he didn't want it to end.

Finally, her hand touched his and, reluctant as all hell, he moved so his palm rested on her tummy, watching it rise and fall, the rhythm matching the heartbeat he felt as he kissed her neck.

"That was so…" She looked into his eyes and grinned full-out.

His laughter must have tickled her, if her little squeal was any indicator. "Natalie," he said, realizing with a jolt that he had no idea what her last name was. "You are amazing."

NATALIE TURNED TO him as she tried to collect herself. The look in his eyes was a little smug and a lot wanting. She felt as loose limbed as a rag doll. "This wasn't anything like…" She stopped, feeling foolish for being embarrassed now. She'd been more out there with Max than any guy she'd ever been with, and it wasn't even midnight. Or maybe it was, she wasn't sure. It didn't matter. "That wasn't what I was expecting," she said, finally. "I mean. It was strong." She gripped his arm, needing him to understand. "So. Much. Better."

"Sweet Natalie," he said, kissing the top of her breast, "that was only the appetizer." His grin made his eyes crinkle, but when his penis brushed against her hip, he winced. And stopped.

Her hand went to his erection. He gasped at the touch. She gasped at the heat and hardness. "Why didn't you…you know…do something…for yourself?"

After a few long seconds when he didn't do anything but bite his lower lip, he let out a gust of air. "I was busy."

"That is so nice." Her palm moved up and down the length of him, not exactly sure how tightly to hold him. Oliver didn't like much pressure, but Tim had preferred a firm hand. She split the difference, and from the way he was straining—the muscles on his neck were a little alarming—she was doing okay.

He grabbed onto her wrist and she froze, but all he did was lie down. She couldn't help leaning over him and giving him a kiss. Sweetly, he returned her kiss but she knew that he needed a lot more. When his eyes opened again and he'd let her go, she continued to stroke him.

Max's eyes widened and he groaned as if in pain. Pausing, she questioned him with a look. His jerky nod came a few seconds later.

Before she began again, she licked her lips, looked down, first at her hand on his cock, then at her breasts, where he was sure to notice that her nipples were still as hard as new pencil erasers. Then she gave him a little squeeze before running a slow hand from base to crown.

One of the things she liked very much about sex was the feel of a penis. That juxtaposition of soft and hard, steel and silk. But men, they liked a little show. It still shocked her that she'd danced in front of him. Her, of all people!

"Uh, Natalie?"

"Yes?"

"As much as I love what you're doing, you need to stop."

She stopped. "You nodded. Did I do something wrong?"

"No," he said, but his voice sounded strained to the limit. "You're too good at this. I don't want to come yet. Appetizer, remember?"

"Oh. Oh." She snatched her hand back. "That doesn't seem very fair."

"Just give me a few minutes, okay? Five, maybe ten. Then we can, you know, continue."

Nodding, she wondered if she should back off entirely. There was so much of him she wanted to touch. Simply watching him breathe was a major turn-on. It wasn't as if he was a bodybuilder or anything. That had never appealed, but the men she'd been with before to-night had all been…soft.

Which hadn't been a problem. She honestly didn't think much about their physiques. But they'd been nothing like Max. Everything about him was toned and sleek. His chest was a lot like his cock—soft skin with no padding. Nothing but hard sinew and muscle underneath.

Her hand hovered over his chest, aching to stroke him from shoulder to thigh, but she held back. "Too soon?"

"Think so. Maybe, uh, maybe you could get us something to drink?"

A quick peek down told her that yeah, he was still impressively rigid. The length of him lay straight up to the middle of his belly, where a little pool of precome had formed just below his navel. A wicked tremor raced through her body, but she ignored it, at least for now. "Cognac? Water? Something else?"

"There's bottled water in the fridge," he said, his eyes closed again. It was entirely too tempting to pet him. He looked so…tense.

She realized as she sat up that she had no robe with her, and putting on her dress seemed weird. But there was his shirt, and lucky her, it smelled like him. A kind of woodsy something that was exactly right. She'd noticed it when she'd sniffed his neck.

The trip to the fridge was over quickly. As soon as she'd opened the door, she wondered if he ate all his meals out. There was plenty of beer, a good supply of water, large jars of chunky peanut butter and straw-berry jam. A loaf of bread was in there, too, as was a knife. Guess when he wanted his PB&J, he wanted it right that second.

On the way back, she slowed her step as she looked around the loft. In any other city, except maybe San Francisco or Tokyo, it would have seemed small. But in Manhattan, where real estate was utterly insane, Max had a veritable palace.

She wondered if it was his or if he sublet. Maybe he came from money, although she didn't get that feeling. She wasn't going to ask. In truth, she didn't want to know too much about him. Except for his body.

If Fred could see her now, he'd have a heart attack. Fred thought her social life was a disaster, except for game nights. Those he loved, but her choice in men? According to Fred, she was stuck in a rut that would lead her into a terrible marriage and a lifetime of regret.

Maybe she could somehow convince Max to take a picture of the two of them together. After they'd gotten dressed again. As proof. So Fred could take his prognostications and shove it.

She stopped at the door to the bedroom. Max's eyes were closed, and while his cock was still hard, it didn't look painful any longer. Good. She wanted another round of his magic before she had to go back to the real world. The thought alone was so unlike her, she shivered.

He turned his head and smiled at her. "I thought you got lost out there."

She held up the bottled water. "I was able to find my way there and back again..."

The image of him sitting up, his bent elbows causing all kinds of wonderful things to stretch on his chest, was another Instagram moment wasted. But she'd remember it.

They both hydrated as she got settled in bed. Before she took off his shirt, she pulled up the top sheet and covered a good portion of herself while trying not to hide much of Max.

"You gonna take off that shirt?" he asked.

"It smells good."

He put his water down and rolled over so his head was in her lap. Gripping her hips, he inhaled deeply. "You make me hungry," he said.

Before she'd even figured out he was being literal, he'd maneuvered himself between her legs and yanked her a good ways down the bed.

"I haven't even taken off your—"

His mouth was on her, his thumbs spreading her wide, his tongue licking her open.

She fell back, thankfully missing the headboard. Not only was the feeling unprecedented, because hell, he was enthusiastic, but it also made her want to go back to every single guy she'd been with, all four of them, and slap them right across the face, just like Loretta had in *Moonstruck* and oh! That was his tongue. His pointed tongue.

In a remarkably short time she came again, hard, like the first time, and before she got her breath back, he'd donned a condom and was leaning over her, one hand by her left ear, bracing himself as he filled her. The angle made his cock rub against her astonishingly sensitive clit and she spasmed. Again.

"Open your eyes," he said, the words constricted behind his clenched teeth.

She hadn't realized she'd closed them.

He was right above her, staring, his face flushed, beads of sweat dotting his brow. It shocked her, how close, how intense, how naked she felt. It was tempting to turn away, but she couldn't. She could barely blink.

Another shock hit her system and she brought her legs up to curl around his slim hips.

"That's it," he said, lifting them a bit higher with his right hand. "This is what you wanted, isn't it? You're hungry for it. I can feel you milking my cock. Don't worry," he said, the words almost lost on a gasp. "You're not done." His thrusts grew deeper and faster, pushing her whole body up the bed. "Come on. I want to see it. Don't close your eyes. Please. Let me watch."

She couldn't obey him. It was too much. The rub wasn't there every time, which made each time it appeared more powerful. People weren't meant to have this much sensation with their eyes open. But when she closed them, when she cried out so loudly it shocked her, he bent down and kissed her. Fast and deep. "Open them, now, Natalie," he said. "Now, because I can feel you getting ready. Your legs and your hips are getting so tense you'll break me in half. That's what I want. Do it," he said, grinding into her. "Come for me. Now. Now."

She shattered. It was as if every part of her was connected to a trigger that had just been pulled. Her mouth opened on a silent scream as she contorted into a shape she didn't recognize.

"That's it. God, that's gorgeous," he said as he went harder, faster.

She opened her eyes again, barely able to see between the white spots in her vision. But his face. Exquisite agony. A low moan built and built until finally he slammed into her and froze. His breath, the air around them, the city. Everything stopped as he came, and she trembled through another quake, an awakening.

# 6

NATALIE RISING BROUGHT Max out of his stupor. He liked the view as she shifted to sit on the edge of the bed, the top sheet held to her chest. Her pale back looked as soft as it felt, but she was so still he resisted touching her.

When she stood, leaving the sheet behind, the view was even better. He could still feel her waist beneath his hands, her firm bottom. He'd wait until she got back from the bathroom to take care of his own business, and then ask her if she wanted to have some cheesecake and milk. Satisfying one hunger had awakened another, and there was every chance the circle could continue after refreshments.

Then she picked up her dress. And her bra. No panties to worry about, which still shocked the hell out of him, but more important, she was getting ready to leave. "Hey," he said.

She jumped a little, now using her dress to cover herself. "I thought you were asleep."

"Nope. Awake and hungry. You know, you don't have to leave this minute. I was going to bring you a piece of cheesecake."

"Sounds yummy," she said, "but I need to go."

"Don't tell me you have to work tomorrow. It's Saturday."

"I do have to. But not until the afternoon. I don't have work days like most people. Officially I take Tuesdays and Thursdays off, and every other Saturday. But that changes almost weekly due to conferences and local events."

"Ah. You must really like what you do." He threw back his part of the sheet. "I'll take you down."

"Don't bother. Honestly. I'm just going to walk over to Broadway and catch a cab."

"Yeah," he said, not rolling his eyes, but wanting to. "It's almost two a.m. No way you're walking by yourself."

She lowered her lashes as she smiled. "Thank you. That's very gallant."

His laugh was more like a bark than he'd care to admit. "Now there's something I've never been accused of before."

Awkwardly keeping herself mostly facing him, she moved toward his bathroom. Before she disappeared, she paused. Sadly, all he could see was her head and one shoulder. "You think being gallant is a bad thing?"

"Not at all. That's what counts for humor at two in the morning. I would like to believe that it's not gallantry so much as common courtesy. I'd hate to see anything happen to you."

"That's nice. Not that many people are courteous these days. I'll be out in a sec."

The door closed and he got up, stretching extravagantly. He pulled out his most comfortable jeans and his Northwestern University sweatshirt. He wouldn't dress until he'd washed up, but with the addition of a pair of socks, he was prepared. He would have preferred putting her into a cab, but the walk wasn't a big deal.

She came out looking pretty damn great. Her hair wasn't as neat, but that was a good look on her.

By the time they were ready to leave, she'd made him put half the cheesecake in his fridge and taken the rest in the box. She accepted the loan of his leather jacket, and then they were outside, the air cool but not uncomfortable.

"Tonight was fun," she said, as they headed for Lafayette. "Unexpected and very educational."

"I'm glad," he said, walking just close enough that they almost touched shoulders. He liked New York at this time of the morning. It wasn't quiet, not by any means, but it was subdued for downtown. The bars hadn't closed yet, but honking wasn't allowed anymore so the never-ending traffic wasn't too much of an intrusion, and the big garbage trucks wouldn't be on their way to his neck of the woods for at least another hour.

"I'm glad, too," she said. "It was a definite step outside my comfort zone, but you made it safe. Thanks for that."

He grinned. "I'm going to call my mom later and tell her she did a good job raising me. She'll be delighted. She'd lost hope by the time I was in high school. Thought I was a selfish brat. Not without reason, I must confess."

"Really? How were you bratty?"

He sighed, not sure he wanted to confess quite so much, but what the hell. It wasn't as if he would see her again. "I got a little carried away. I thought I was hot, and a lot of the girls in my school agreed. It wasn't pretty, actually. I was the farthest thing from gallant you can imagine."

"Teenage hormones. Understood."

"My brother, Mike, wasn't quite such an ass."

"Was he close to your age?" she asked, looking pretty under the streetlight.

"About four minutes younger. So the comparison was apt. And shoved down my throat. The 'why can't you be more like your brother?' had a lot to do with my issues."

"You have a twin." She looked startled, and then smiled as if she'd just remembered something. "Identical?"

"Yep. You find this amusing?"

She shook her head. "Is he on a trading card?" she asked. "Not for me. My friend made a remark—never mind." She cleared her throat. "Are you two close now?"

"Yeah. He lives just outside of Oyster Bay. I haven't seen him a lot lately because of work. He recently opened an art gallery in Sag Harbor."

"It must be nice, having a twin. I assume you still aren't being compared to him unfavorably?"

Max chuckled. "Nah, we're good. What about you? You a native New Yorker?"

"Yeah, I am," she said, and then she winced.

"What's wrong?"

"High heels are the devil's work is what's wrong. I'd rather be thinking about the lovely night and not my aching feet."

"Yeah, I'm enjoying the walk, myself. But if you're in pain—"

"The ridiculous part is that my house is so close. I'm in the Bowery, by Sheriff. Amusingly, I live on Attorney Street."

"That is close. Huh. No wonder we ate at Lviv."

"Family," she said and shrugged.

"Makes perfect sense." They'd stopped, and she'd used his shoulder for balance as she'd taken off her left shoe. He liked the way she wiggled her toes. The dark maroon nails looked black between lampposts. "I've got an idea."

"What's that?" She switched to the other shoe, and commenced the wiggle.

"We're really close to some benches. Why don't we go sit down for a little, give your feet a rest, then let's see if you want to walk the rest of the way or not."

Her grin was great, and that they would spend a little more time together was kind of nice. He liked her. Not enough to change their arrangement, but for his first night back in the thick of things, Natalie had been a terrific mistake.

It didn't take them long to get to the metal benches, a rare commodity in Manhattan, especially finding two of the four empty. They sat as far from the others as possible, and he leaned back to put his arm on the back rest above her shoulders.

"I wish we had forks," she said, staring at the box on her lap.

"I swear, I'll never tell another living soul if you want to sneak a bite with your fingers."

She arched an eyebrow at him. "Eating cheesecake right out of the box is no trifling matter. My reputation could be ruined."

"Fair enough," he said. "To seal my pact of silence, I'll have a bite myself. Maybe even two."

"You rogue. Deal."

She flipped the lid back, and his mouth got a little too excited. "Ladies first," he said. Now that was gallant.

Her giggling softly and him enjoying her unabashed enthusiasm, they both managed a few messy tastes each and ended the treat the only way they could, sucking the confection off their fingers. Watching her reminded him of their recent activities, and yep, little Max made it known he was ready and willing.

Big Max just crossed his legs, relaxed against the bench and put his arm around Natalie's shoulders.

NATALIE SHOULD HAVE been far more concerned than she was. The whole night with the wrong Max had felt more right than any date she'd ever had. After she'd done such a good job getting out of his bed and getting dressed, she'd caved the second he'd suggested the walk.

A smart woman would have cut things off at his loft. It was bad enough she could never go to Trattoria Spaghetto again, given the memories and associations, but the entire path from NoHo to the Bowery? It would make her miserable, at least for a while. But then she'd meet Max Zimm, and all would be right with the world.

She looked at the Max by her side and her optimism came crashing down to earth. Things would be all right, but after having danced with the prince at the ball, it would be hard to go back to the valet. Realistically, although she wanted to call the real Max Zimm right away, she'd need to wait until the glow from tonight diminished. Would Max Zimm still be available? Possibly not, but she wasn't going to regret tonight. She'd accept the consequences and hope for the best.

"That is one serious expression you've got," Max said. "Anything wrong?"

"Nope," she said, putting on a happier visage. "I'm surprised I feel so awake, frankly."

He nodded. "You mentioned you pack it in on the early side."

"I like mornings," she said. "I have a small balcony outside my bedroom. I've put a table and chair out there, and I like to watch the sunrise while I enjoy my morning coffee."

Max smiled gently. "That's completely insane. Nobody does that in real life."

"Who said I live in the real world? I've been stuck in the movies most of my life. Come on, tell me you can't picture the scene. Not in winter, obviously, but to be there when a city this vibrant awakens? It's glorious."

"No one says *glorious* either, for the record. What floor do you live on that has this spectacular view?"

"The second. All right, I don't watch the whole city. But I do watch my street come to life. That's fun. Also, I totally see naked people across the street. Through their windows. Don't know why they don't close the blinds more often, but they don't."

"They? What is it, a co-op for exhibitionists?"

"I don't think so. There are only a couple of reliable windows. One with a couple in their mid-thirties, I'd guess. She's in great shape, and he's not bad, either. I can't see their bed, just the short distance between that and the bathroom. Sometimes it's too dark, but most often, they switch on the bathroom light before they close the door."

"Wow, you really are a Peeping Tom." His brow furrowed. "Peeping Tina." That didn't please him, either. "Perv. That's the word I'm looking for."

She hit his thigh. "I'm sure you'd be a total gentleman and never once peek."

"Oh, I'd have the best binoculars money could buy."

"Ah. Then I'm in good company."

Max's laugh made her giddy. The whole silly conversation had. "No comment," he said.

"As much as I'm enjoying this, I really should go home. Let you get some sleep as well."

"I'm in no rush. How're the feet?"

"Okay. You'd think I'd know better than to let beauty win over practicality. Most of my heels are sensible. Comfy." She lifted her legs to look at the black five inchers that were determined to kill her. Sighing grandly, she looked at Max. "They were on sale. Fifty percent off."

"Those bastards," he said.

"Exactly." She laughed. "Something else, for the record? I can't believe I just told you that."

Squeezing her shoulder, he leaned over to kiss her lightly on the lips. It was nothing like the searing drama of their earlier make-out session, but it still made her heart pound and her cheeks heat.

"Want me to catch you a cab, or should we be stalwart troopers and walk the rest of the way?"

"Nice. Make me feel like a wimp if I say no."

"That wasn't my intention," he said, his gaze and hers so locked on each other, East Houston could have crumbled and she wouldn't have noticed. "Although I'll admit, I'd like to see you to your door."

"Really?"

He nodded.

"Are you just trying to get the address of the nude couple across the way?"

His wince was exaggerated and adorable. "Man, I thought we had an understanding about the whole pervert business."

"Sorry. My fault. Let's brave the mean streets and get me home. I might even give you another bite of cheesecake."

He stood, held out his hand for her, the smile he was trying to control hinting that his mind had gone in the wrong direction.

She gave him the opportunity to drop her hand once she was standing, but he didn't. Not there, not all the way to Attorney, where she pointed out the building in question, then her own redbrick home.

"You own the building?" he asked, so surprised he stopped completely before they'd reached her steps.

"My parents bought it years ago. I rent out the bottom floor, which I've converted into a separate apartment. It pays most of my taxes, and I figure when it's time, I'll sell the old place and move into something smaller. Where I don't have to be the landlord."

"Wow, smart planning. Very wise. So your parents are…?"

"My father passed away in 1998. My mother's alive and well and living in sin with her boyfriend, Solomon, in Brooklyn."

"Living in sin?" Max shook his head as he bumped her shoulder with his own. "It's been really fun talking to you."

"Oh." She hadn't expected such an abrupt goodbye. Admittedly, she was safe here, steps away from home, but still.

"No, I mean that literally. It's a pleasure to talk to you. You're bright and witty and there hasn't been a hint of legalese since dinner. I can't tell you how refreshing it's been."

"Oh," she repeated, but in a completely different way. "I'm glad. It has been fun. For all kinds of reasons."

"Yes," he said, serious now, no teasing in his eyes or the way he held himself. "Altogether a memorable night."

She looked at her house, knowing she had no business even thinking of inviting him anywhere close to it, but she didn't want the spell to end quite yet. Turning back, she held up the box of cheesecake. "I wasn't kidding about helping me with this. It's late. My defenses are down. I need more cheesecake like I need a bunion."

"I have excellent taste in cheesecake," he said. "Shoot me."

"Let me keep that option in reserve," she said, and he grinned. "Instead, why don't you come in? I'll make coffee. I make very good coffee."

"It's pretty late for coffee," he said, but she could see he was thinking about it.

"I make good decaf, too."

"Sure. I've been fighting off stealing that box for a good five blocks."

Showing her good faith in him, she let him hold the prize until she got her keys out. He held the door for her, and as soon as she crossed the threshold, Fred's strident voice said, "Where the hell have you been, and why haven't you answered your... Oh, hel-lo."

The surprised look on Max's face was one she'd remember for a long, long time. Sadly, she would remember all the other looks, too. Each and every one.

# 7

"MAX, THIS IS FRED. He lives here. And despite appearances, he's not my dad or my conscience."

Max relaxed into an offered handshake, but his smile was met with narrowed eyes. Fred was tall and thin, with dark reddish hair and a long face dominated at the moment by a look of suspicion.

"You're the trading-card guy." It didn't sound much like a question.

He caught a glimpse of Natalie's grin as she shook her head.

"Sort of."

Fred looked from him to her and back. "Meaning…?"

"Right picture, wrong bio."

"How'd that happen?"

Natalie slipped out of her heels. "Printing glitch. But it turned out to be a nice evening anyway. I'm making coffee," she said pointedly at Max. "Still want some?"

"It's after two in the morning," Fred said, at the exact time Max said, "You know what?"

Natalie's expression fell. "It is late."

Max stepped closer to her and touched the back of her elbow. He hesitated to go upstairs, mostly because he wanted to. But it didn't seem like a good idea. Fred's presence had brought Natalie's life into focus in a way her family at Lviv hadn't. Probably because he knew her better now. Tonight was truly a one-off, an outlier for her. She was on a trajectory that suited her, with her safety net of friends and relatives around her. He didn't fit, and her protective tenant had seen that immediately.

Behind him, Fred cleared his throat. "I'll catch up with you tomorrow, Nat."

Natalie had her focus squarely on Max. "Yeah, okay."

Fred's door closing made the whole goodbye easier. First, Max slipped the box of cheesecake out of her hand so he could put it on the stairs. Then he moved closer so he could run his hands down both her arms. "I should go," he said. "It's been a great night. Thank you."

She inhaled and gave him a quick nod. "You, too. I could never have imagined the evening turning out the way it has. If you had any idea what I'm like normally, you'd be more than shocked. But as far as mistakes go, you've been top-notch."

"Then it was a success for both of us."

It was a perfect exit line, and yet, he hesitated just long enough that he couldn't hold back from leaning in for a last kiss. Even that was meant to be short and sweet. Instead, the second he felt her lips part, he slipped inside. Her soft whimper combined with her hands on the back of his neck set him in motion.

He pulled her tight against him as he guided her back and back until she was against the wall. They kissed as if they'd been practicing for ages, the ebb and flow, small partings that led to different angles and stolen breaths.

When his hand moved to her shoulder, on its way to the silk of her breast beneath that red dress, he stopped. Not just his hand, but his kiss, the way he pressed his half-hard cock against her dress.

She blinked up at him.

He studied her eyes in the light from the overhead lamp before he stepped back. He couldn't see much of the house from this small foyer. A staircase with a dark wood banister, green-and-white fleur-de-lis wallpaper that seemed exactly right for the woman still in his arms. A light-year away from anything in his world. "I'm gonna..." He gave a nod at the front door.

She smiled, and her cheeks pinked up. "Please be careful on the way home. In fact, take a cab. You can get one easily on Houston."

"Thanks. I will." He let her go, and after the door closed behind him, he let the night go. It had been an interesting detour, but now he was on back on his own road.

NATALIE KNOCKED TWICE. "You can come out now."

Fred's door opened so fast it made her jump. He had to have been standing there with his ear pressed to the wood. "Jesus, woman," he said. "When you decide you're not going out with anyone like Oliver Feinstein, you don't mess around."

She sighed. "There's no way I'm falling asleep yet. Come up and have Italian cheesecake with me."

He turned his head to look back at his room, and then marched right by her to the stairs. "You still have that bottle of Crown Royal you got for Christmas last year?"

"I do, although I shouldn't give you any. I saw you steal my beer."

"I'll buy you more when I go to the store. So tell me how this all came about." He reached her floor and waited impatiently for her to open it, peeking inside the box she thrust in his hand.

Once inside, Natalie flicked on the light and dropped

her shoes by the coatrack and went straight into her long galley kitchen. She gathered the whiskey, two glasses and two forks, and met Fred at the table parked at the end of the room. After shoving everything but her fork toward him, she stared at what was left of the decadent cheesecake and knew she wouldn't be able to eat a bite. That alone told her she might be in for trouble. Even worse, if Fred noticed... She tried not to whimper.

"Okay, now you're making sex noises, and I thought we agreed never to do that." He'd poured the whiskey and was digging in to the dessert.

She simply waited, taking a small piece of cake to avoid unwanted questions.

Fred was making yummy noises, but then he pointed his fork at her and said, "Enough foreplay. Tell me what happened tonight."

She began at the beginning. The restaurant, the revelation, the aborted escape. On to restaurant two, the conversation, the dessert invitation...

Fred knew her well, and when she stopped talking, he stared at her with equal parts disbelief and *oh, my God.* "You didn't."

She pressed her lips together.

"Holy shit!" His gaze still locked on her, he shoveled in another forkful. "It's too late to play coy now," he said. "What's his place like?"

"Sort of what you'd expect." She shrugged, deciding how much she wanted to tell him. "Giant TV, masculine colors. Big, but nearly empty. It's a loft, a nice one. Had to have cost a bundle even if he'd bought it during the days of real-estate bingo."

Fred looked at her as if the debate team were having it out in his head. "I can't express how much I never wanted to know anything about your relationship with

Oliver. There simply aren't words. And since I'm not actually your best girlfriend, it's probably inappropriate as hell for me to ask now. But was he amazing? He looked like he'd be amazing."

She felt herself blush for what had to be the hundredth time tonight. She and Fred were really close. He was like the brother she'd always wanted. But they'd never gone into details about intimate things. Of course she knew his history, that although he'd been single for a couple of years, he wasn't anymore. His longtime friend Tony had become something more.

Which didn't change the fact that she and Fred filled the void for each other where more outgoing people would have a bunch of friends, people they'd call to go shopping or to movies or concerts. She knew a lot of librarians and archivists, but the only one who came close to being a real friend was Denise. They saw each other at book and film events and sometimes socially. But they were content to catch up with each other when it felt right and not just for the sake of touching base.

It would cross a boundary, telling Fred more than she had. But this was evidently her night to leap. "Amazing doesn't even come close," she said, her cheeks reheating epically. She could have roasted marshmallows on them.

"Good for you." Fred squeezed her hand and smiled his real smile, the one that was a little asymmetrical, but endearing. The one he rarely showed in public.

"It was terrifying. I hardly believed it was me."

"I'm so glad. You had to get Oliver's fingerprints off you once and for all. Not just Oliver. You don't need to settle. You're a fantastic person. You don't think enough of yourself, Nat, and it's a shame."

"Look who's talking."

Fred wasn't grinning any longer. "I know. It's how I can recognize it clearly in you."

"Well, this got awfully deep, awfully fast."

"Sorry," he said, pushing the remaining quarter of the cheesecake toward her.

"It's fine. I honestly don't mind. But you do realize this was a one-night thing. I'm not going to see Max again."

Leaning back in his chair, Fred shook his head as he pulled out his oft-used puzzled expression. "That's not the vibe I got."

"It's the vibe that was there. Trust me. The only reason I was able to go for it was because I'd never see him again. Seriously, he's into one-night stands and staying single."

"Please, please tell me this wasn't sleazy. He wasn't condescending or acting like he was doing you a favor, was he?"

"God, no. Not even. I wasn't kidding when I said we had a great time together. It was the best date I've ever had, bar none. Because we were honest with each other. We both had plenty of opportunities to walk away with no regrets. He was a gentleman, and he was quite attentive."

"Okay. Just checking. It's a rough city out there."

"Thanks for worrying, but no. It was inspiring and illuminating and he's probably ruined me for other men. At least for a while. I don't mind, though. It was worth it, if for nothing else but to show me what to ask for. What to reach for."

"An attorney with a big loft?"

"A man who gets pleasure from giving it. A man who pays attention and goes out of his way to be careful. Who listens."

"Okay." Fred got up, pushed his chair in and finished the last dregs of his whiskey. "Does this trading-card thing have a gay edition?"

"No, but that's a fabulous idea. You should start one."

"Yeah. I'll get right on that. Think you can sleep?"

"Nope. Maybe. But I don't have to get up until ten-thirty. If I'm willing to have the quickest shower in history."

"I hate to tell you, sweetheart, but even if you conk out when your head hits the pillow, you're not going to get your regular eight."

"Regular eights are for ordinary days. I'll live."

He kissed her cheek. "You did good tonight. That inspiration thing is catching. Although I'm happy with Tony for now."

She looked up at her friend. "I'm glad."

Fred eyed the cheesecake and her clean fork with a worried look. Thankfully he just smiled and headed for the stairs. Cleanup was a snap, but when she finally crawled between her sheets, the night and alcohol caught up with her, and before she'd even finished reliving the way Max had looked at her over dinner, she slipped into sleep.

On Sunday, Max was still in recuperation mode. At least today he wouldn't be fielding phone calls from his office, headhunters trying to convince him to jump ship. Not that he minded the second category of calls.

He'd planned on going to his local bar, but his couch had proven too comfortable. Surprisingly, his inertia had more to do with his night with Natalie than laziness. The odds of meeting someone as interesting were not in his favor.

As often as he'd daydreamed about having time to

himself without the crushing pressure of the tort case, unstructured down time wasn't his friend. He should have realized it. He was a planner, always thinking about the next move, the next angle. He was damn good at scheduling his life so he didn't get overwhelmed.

Until the second year of the case, that was. His enormous workload didn't leave him with a spare moment to do anything besides sleep, eat and work out—and he'd finally hit a wall. The workouts were the only thing that saved him.

That was probably why he felt so out of sync now. Tomorrow he'd go back to the gym, get his blood pumping and his muscles straining. It wouldn't take him long to find his rhythm again. While he didn't regret spending an idle week in recovery, the next two weeks were earmarked for getting serious about his future. In the legal arena, he was the it guy of the moment, which was great for his ego, but he couldn't let it get to him. A man who let his ego call the shots was looking for trouble. Luckily for him, his inherent need to plan and control his own destiny would keep him in check.

He'd always known there was the potential for a top-notch lawyer in a prominent firm to make big money. He simply hadn't realized how big. Not until he'd earned a spot at the heavy hitters' table. The dollar figures being thrown around were ridiculous. Enough to tempt anyone. Whether he stayed with his firm or went elsewhere, he'd have it made financially. But he'd be expected to work his ass off. Normal people didn't stay at the office past ten every single night. He shuddered to think of the divorce rate in the legal community. And that was the other thing. Someday—not soon, but someday—he wanted a family.

For now the hard work wasn't a problem. That didn't

mean he was willing to trade the rest of his life for a fat bank account and a corner office. His love of the law had always been his motivation to become an attorney. And making good money and having nice things, like his loft, his expensive suits and a great wine collection, sure helped.

It was a great deal, actually. He'd become accustomed to nice things. Between the cash and the flattery, it was tough to stay centered and make the right decision. If he got a bad vibe from a firm, no sweat, he'd turn down even the most extravagant offer. But whether he should stay with Latham or jump ship was a lot more complicated. He'd be dealing with some of the smoothest talkers in the world. Despite the treacherous road ahead, he was ready to get off his ass and start the ball rolling. Talking himself up wasn't his favorite thing, but he could do it when it counted. Hell, he'd had the perfect opportunity to brag about his accomplishments to Natalie. After all, the case had been all over the papers. But he hadn't said a word to her about it.

Natalie.

He thought about her quite a lot. He'd discovered that a film she'd talked about was on the tube tonight. It was called *M.* Just *M,* and it was about to begin. Although he'd known it was shot in black and white, he hadn't realized it was in German with subtitles. That would mean paying attention, and he wasn't sure he had it in him. But he'd give it a few minutes.

A few minutes was all it took to get him hooked. The opening scene was more ominous and gripping than anything he'd seen in ages. The only thing missing was popcorn, and wait, he had some microwave bags in the kitchen.

It took him twenty minutes to find a place he was

willing to pause, and as he pressed the magical popcorn button on his built-in microwave, he thanked whoever had invented the DVR.

Then he thought about Natalie again. About how he'd gotten off to the memory of her doing that crazy little dance for him. And how he'd felt when her legs had wrapped around his waist.

The microwave beeped, and he didn't bother with a bowl, but he did grab a beer. It would have been fun to watch the movie with her. He considered calling her, but that wouldn't be smart. Not in the long run. She was actively looking for a husband, and he didn't want to mess with that.

He'd been an experiment and now she was back in her own orbit. The end. Pity, though, because he'd enjoyed her company. He didn't have many people in his life he could say that about. Not anymore.

On the other hand, Natalie was a grown-up and she could make her own decisions. He might call her, although not this minute. Maybe after the movie. He wouldn't mind watching it a second time with her.

The popcorn was good, but it wouldn't hold him. Max left the movie on pause so he could order takeout curry from Spice Thai on Astor. Just as he picked up his phone, it rang. It was his cousin Paula. He'd left her a message on Saturday about the mix-up with the cards.

"I'm so sorry," she said after they'd exchanged hellos.

"It's okay. It turned out fine."

"This shouldn't have happened," Paula said. "The woman who runs the printing company has already made new cards—with the correct pictures this time— but listen, how would you feel about me preemptively setting you up with someone? I really think you'll like her, and vice versa. She's not in the market for a relationship, she's hot and she's smart. She looks a little like Rihanna. You know, the singer?"

"Yeah, I know the singer. You're not messing with me, are you?"

"Nope. Her name is Gabbie and she's joining the Trading Card group because she wants someone who won't turn out to be a whack job. So if you do this thing, you'd better be on your best behavior."

"I'm always on my best behavior," he said.

Paula's laughter was kind of insulting, but he let it pass. Because this was the real beginning of the buffet he'd been promised. Rihanna was smokin' hot, and Paula wasn't the type to exaggerate.

"Okay," she said. "I'll give her your cell number. She's set Tuesday night aside, so you'll just have time to make a reservation. Someplace good."

"You want to come over and pick out my clothes, too?"

"Ha-ha. Just remember, this one's going to be the last one until the next meeting, which isn't for almost a month."

He smiled at her concern and wondered if she'd mentioned the trading-card business to Mike, or her folks, because yeah, this was the kind of thing that could end up in his aunt Ellen's Christmas newsletter if they weren't careful. "I'll buy you lunch next week. You've gone to a lot of trouble for something that wasn't your fault."

"You're right. Call me."

He hung up, figured he'd get moving and go to Spice. Despite the lack of structure in his life, things were going pretty damn well. He'd just received an invitation to a cocktail party at one of the top twenty law firms in the country. Which was a very big deal. Then there'd been the date with Natalie, and that had turned out to be great. Now this.

He hoped Gabbie turned out to be as advertised, because it might have been an error, but Natalie had set the bar pretty high. At least he knew that his next date wouldn't want anything he couldn't provide.

# 8

MONDAYS AT OMNIBUS Film Archives were always busy, but with two back-to-back tours and an afternoon screening of Buñuel's *L'Age d'Or* for a class of film students, Natalie would be lucky if she got any kind of a break at all.

She'd had to fight the urge to daydream about Friday night, but both her coworker Veda, and her boss, Rick, had given her funny looks, so she knew she wasn't exactly winning the battle. Of course she wouldn't even give them a hint as to her thoughts. Everyone who was on staff, all dozen of them, knew that she'd been with Oliver for three years, and Natalie hadn't told anyone they'd split up.

It was a friendly group, constantly busy because they could have used at least a dozen more full-timers, with a budget that barely paid the ones they had. So they hired interns and part-timers, almost exclusively students from colleges and universities around the city.

Their days were packed and they traded workdays and hours, especially evenings and weekends when they held screenings, fund-raisers and classes. When the staff socialized, they tended to talk shop. There wasn't much gossip at Omnibus. This morning's tour was part of a program offered by the American Association of

Retired Persons. There were also a few other people taking part, including Elizabeth Carter, a PhD student who researched there often. Elizabeth loved the tour, but mostly she liked to play Stump the Librarian when Natalie was leading the group, which was fine because Natalie enjoyed the game, as well.

They were standing outside the basement lab at the moment, crowded around the large window to watch the work going on inside. Once all eleven people on the tour were as well situated as possible, Natalie began her spiel. "Sadly, movies aren't made to last. Almost all old films were made of perishable plastic, which decays within years if not properly stored. Only twenty percent of U.S. feature films from the 1910s and 1920s survive in their complete form. We make sure that movies will be here to be studied and enjoyed for years to come."

As always, she met the gazes of as many people as she comfortably could to keep the conversation engaging even through the technical parts. But a motion from down the hallway caught her attention. At first she thought she saw Max, but that wasn't possible. A second look proved her wrong.

Whatever she'd been saying was lost as she watched him approach. He wore jeans, a dark blue polo shirt and a smile. She wondered if she'd forgotten something at his loft.

By the time he reached the group, everyone was staring at him. His smile dimmed and his step faltered. "I was told I could join the tour even though I'm late. Is that okay?"

Now all eyes were on Natalie. She opened her mouth and then stood there mutely as she tried to get a grip. Finally, she nodded. It took several more seconds for her to say, "If you'd like to, that's fine. We were just talking about film preservation."

"Great," he said. "Thanks. Sorry for the interruption."

Natalie tried to force herself to focus on the task at hand and scrambled to reconnect with her core eleven. "Saving films is expensive. In, uh, 2011, no 2010, it cost almost twenty thousand dollars to remaster a seven-reel black-and-white silent feature. That's not counting any special restoration work. Creating a digital video for public viewing adds another three grand to the total. Preserving a movie with sound can cost—uh…"

She knew this. She'd given the same talk at least a hundred times in the two and a half years she'd worked there.

"From fifty to one hundred thousand dollars," Elizabeth said, making her way toward Natalie. When she got close, she whispered, "If you need to speak to your friend, I can take over."

"Oh, no. He's just… I don't… I should…"

"Go. I promise I won't screw up, and this'll look good on my résumé." Elizabeth turned her attention to the group. "Do you mind if I fill in for a bit? I'm doing my PhD on film preservation, and though I'll never be as accomplished as Natalie, I promise not to make things up."

The tour group responded with gentle laughter and seemingly approved, so Natalie nodded. "Thanks. I'll be back soon." Then she turned to Max. He looked as if he was about to bolt. She gestured for him to join her, and they didn't speak until they arrived at the elevator that led to the lobby and her office. When the doors closed and the old Otis began its journey up, he cleared his throat.

"I'm sorry I interrupted."

"It's okay. Really. Elizabeth is very capable of leading the tour. She'll probably end up working here."

Upon exiting the elevator, they were greeted by old movie posters that dotted the brick walls of the lobby. The building's high ceilings carried the sound of their footsteps as they walked down the long hallway to her office.

"I won't keep you," he said as he looked around her office and then at her. "I have no idea why I thought it was a good idea to walk in without calling first. I was just down the street—"

"It's fine," she said and took a seat in one of the guest chairs while he sat in the other. "Honestly. I don't mind at all. But I am curious as to why you're here."

"I saw *M* last night. The Fritz Lang movie."

"Really?"

"You'd mentioned it, and there it was on TV. It was great. Really great, and creepy as hell. I liked that it was in black and white. The shadows. Man. I wanted to talk to you about it. Maybe over dinner tonight?"

Natalie's heart had been racing since she'd caught sight of Max, but now it was trying to pound out of her chest. He wanted to take her to dinner. She hadn't dared dream of such a thing.

"I know I'm breaking the rules," he said, studying her closely.

"Rules?"

"Yeah, the one-night thing?"

"Oh, right." She shrugged and gave him a shaky smile. "It's okay."

"Good." He exhaled. "Because I looked up some stuff about Lang on Wikipedia, and that got me interested in seeing more films like that, and since you're an expert, I thought we could talk about it over some food."

"Huh. That's great. It's always a thrill when someone gets turned on like that. To old movies, I mean. It's such a rich field of study. You mentioned dinner?" She doubted she'd ever been this awkward before. "What time?"

"Six?"

"It's going to have to be closer to seven—" The buzzer on her desk sounded like a foghorn in the small room. Had it always been this loud? "Excuse me."

She picked up the phone. It was Rick. "Why is there a student taking our group on a tour?"

"It's only for few minutes, and she knows the spiel by heart." Natalie turned toward the wall, but in the mirror above her chair, she could see Max stand. Behind him was her mint-condition framed print of Betty Grable as a pinup girl. The sight made her blush. "I had an unexpected visitor."

"Okay," Rick said. "Just wondering."

"I'm wrapping things up right now."

Rick gave his standard goodbye grunt.

Max was already at her door. "I'm off. I'll text you later, okay? We'll work out the details."

"Please don't be concerned. My boss was just checking. He's a great guy, and he doesn't care so much as worry that everyone's okay."

"Good," Max said. "Tell him I won't make the same mistake again. Next time, I'll call first and join a tour for real."

Next time? She tried to keep her cool and succeeded for the most part, although her grin might have given too much away. "I'll walk you out."

"That's okay. I promise to go directly to the lobby."

"I have to walk there anyway."

His chin dropped to his chest. "Good thing I'm a savvy New York attorney or I'd be embarrassed about this."

She laughed. "If it makes you feel any better, all you're doing is evening the score."

He bumped her shoulder, a now-familiar gesture that filled her tummy with butterflies as they walked. "You know what? It does. Thanks."

At the elevator, he didn't linger, and she didn't have to wait, so the goodbye was short. At least the ride back down was private and slow, so she could freak out without being seen.

A second date! Who would have imagined? She'd been so certain he wouldn't want to see her again, and here he'd walked to her office and sought her out in person. And that was after watching a film she'd recommended. She settled for a squeak instead of shouting as the elevator bumped to a halt. Then she stepped back into tour guide mode. It worked...until she got within two feet of the tour group and remembered the polka-dot panties. Tonight she would take no chances. After work she'd go to a real lingerie store and make sure she not only matched, but looked as fabulous as she could. She knew just the place.

WHEN MAX ARRIVED home, he figured he should probably pick up his dry cleaning from the place around the corner. Lord knew it had been awhile since he'd dropped it off. After Max paid his bill, the owner of the cleaners, Mr. Nadeau, warned him that if he used their business as a storage closet again, Max would be banned for life. It was the third or fourth time he'd received the warning, and he hadn't meant to leave his suits and shirts for so long, but his life had gotten so out of control that even something as vital as laundry got skipped in favor of sleep.

Hopefully, this next step in his career would afford him more access to interns. It was an evil system, using those college kids for every kind of grunt work. Back when he was the one sent out to pay parking tickets, stand in line for theater tickets, pick up everything from flowers to jewelry to new curtains, he'd sworn he'd never support that kind of slave labor. The last three years had made him rethink his stance on the practice.

His hypocrisy rankled for a minute before disappearing at the sight of a beautiful woman walking toward him on the busy street. She was exactly his type. Tall and willowy, but not skeletal, her confidence shining as brightly as her hair.

As they passed each other, she gave him a nod of approval, and he returned her acknowledgment with a wolfish smile. A variation on the secret handshake that was just another part of his charmed life. On any other day, he would have turned around and asked her out for coffee, but he didn't want to be late meeting Natalie.

He'd gone through a phase of feeling guilty about his luck. He'd been born to a middle-class family, inherited his good looks and a relatively high IQ. But it hadn't made sense to feel rotten about it. He could only be responsible for what he did with his good fortune, not for having it in the first place.

At the corner of Delancey and Bowery, he pulled out his cell phone and called Natalie. He still didn't understand why he'd made such a mess of things earlier. Why he'd thought it would be okay to barge into her work like that. Maybe because the building was open to the public? Or maybe it was his nerves. He had that cocktail party to go to at nine, and he still wasn't sure if he wanted to leave his firm. He honestly didn't think it was complacency on his part. It was a simple matter of needing more time to figure out what was best for his career.

For now, though, all he really cared about was that Natalie had agreed to have dinner with him. They would eat and get involved in what he hoped would be a fascinating discussion. In fact, he was counting on it. That way, he would not only forget about the cocktail party, but seeing Natalie again, without tonight being a date, per se, could be the beginning of a friendship.

"Hello?" she said, before the third ring. It was noisy on her end as well as his own, the sound of the city an unmistakable soundtrack.

"Hey," he said. "How about trying again at Lviv? I feel like I missed out on something interesting when we bolted."

She didn't answer straightaway. When she did, she sounded hesitant. "Sure. That'd be fine. You do realize the family will probably be annoying."

"I don't mind if you don't. But if you'd prefer to go elsewhere, that's okay. I should warn you that I have to be somewhere at nine, so if we could stick to the Lower East Side or midtown, that would be good."

Again, there was a sizable chunk of ambient noise before she spoke. "No, Lviv is fine," she said finally. "In fact, I'll call ahead. Let them know we'll be there at seven, but we need to be out of there by what, eight-thirty?"

"Yeah, around there. You sure it's okay with you? Seriously, I don't mind a change of venue."

"No, don't worry about it. I'll make sure you get to try some of the more interesting dishes."

"That sounds perfect," he said, but had to practically scream at this point because of a siren. "I'll see you at seven?"

"Yes," she shouted back. "Bye."

That accomplished, he was free to think about the cocktail party after. It was the first of four he'd been invited to, all held by partners in rival law firms. Tonight, he'd be meeting with Beckingham & Quail, who'd won more tort cases than Latham, Kirkland and Jones. The gathering was ostensibly for the firm's fifteenth anniversary, but Max had been assured that he was going to be the main attraction.

His recruiter, Stella, had given him a rundown on what would go down at Parlor, a private club, and who the main players were. He was as prepared as he could be, given the stakes, but he didn't want to overthink the situation.

That was why seeing Natalie beforehand was such a great idea. She'd ground him. Make sure his head was on straight before he was seduced by promises that may or may not come true.

THERE WASN'T A candle on the table this time. Natalie had called ahead and explained to her aunt Hanna that tonight would be a brief dinner with a friend. Nothing more.

She'd thought about changing out of her new underwear after she and Max had talked. But the truth was, there was no one else to wear it for anyway, Thinking about how much money she'd spent on the stupid lingerie, she sighed, and kept watching for Max. He'd be walking through the door any minute, and she had to quit obsessing over the fact that she'd been so wrong about things.

In the hour since Max's call, she'd climbed all the way up the chastisement ladder, settling somewhere between being an unrealistic dreamer and a delusional idiot. Instead, as she surreptitiously adjusted the back strap of her very expensive, gorgeous bra, she pondered the idea of having Max as a friend.

It should have been appealing in every way, but it wasn't. Not when she was so attracted to him. Not when he'd turned her sexual world upside down. It would be like playing with a tiger—very dangerous to her well-being.

So they'd talk about *M* and sample some Ukrainian specialties, and she'd try to end the evening feeling better than she did now. Thank goodness he had to leave at eight-thirty. It would leave her with plenty of time afterward to go home and lick her wounds.

Behind her, from the kitchen, she heard Victor and his arch nemesis, her cousin Ivan, who also owned a Ukrainian restaurant, argue. It got louder as a waiter walked through to the dining room, and dimmed again as the kitchen door settled back into place.

Their table was closer to the kitchen than she'd like, even though there wasn't a customer in the restaurant who wouldn't hear at least some of the argument. She also knew that no one likely cared. At least, none of the regulars. Her crazy family had been quarreling since before they'd left the old country and they'd never stopped. They didn't give a damn who heard, and she normally tuned it out. She really shouldn't have agreed to come back here. Oh, well, she'd warned him…

Max entered the restaurant.

He wore an impeccably tailored suit. The dark navy set off his eyes, and the white shirt, undone at the collar, set off his amazing face perfectly. Whatever he had going on after dinner had to be important.

Probably a date.

The thought made her breath catch.

No, Max wouldn't be that callous. Although if he only considered her a friend...

She had to stop. Just stop. She forced a smile. Not just a smile, but one that matched his greeting. Easy, friendly.

As he got closer, a wellspring of memories shot through her. The pizza, the walk, the polka-dot panties, the thrill, the hope, the letting go. It seemed impossible that she could have such strong connections to a single night. And here he was again, nothing like the man she was looking for. Just the man she didn't dare want.

Before he sat, he kissed her cheek and gave her a quick once-over. She hadn't dressed up. She'd thought of wearing the outfit she'd had on at Omnibus, but instead she'd chosen one just like it. Black pants, royal-green silk button-down, black jacket slung over the back of the chair. The only thing new about her was hidden, beneath her clothes. Beneath her smile.

"I really am sorry about this afternoon. I'm not usually such a dope." He put his napkin on his lap and took a sip of water. "I'm so glad you were free tonight. I've been thinking of that movie all day."

"It's a great film," she said. "I—"

The voices from the kitchen intruded. Loudly. Max looked startled and more than a little concerned as he stared at the swinging door behind her cousin Zoya.

"Don't be alarmed," Natalie said. "That's just my uncle Victor and his brother-in-law Ivan. They both own restaurants, they both come from the same village and they both think the other stole their recipe for cholent. They argue about it every time they're together. Everyone who comes to Lviv or the Litvak has heard this routine a thousand times."

He stared at her as the voices became almost operatic in their shouting. "The food must be fantastic here."

Natalie laughed, and it was as if the heaviness that had bowed her since his phone call had lifted. Okay, so maybe *friend* could be allowed back on the table. "It is. Both of them are incredible cooks. So are their wives, but to them it's not life or death."

"So, can I order this infamous dish? What was it, chent?"

"Cholent," she repeated. "It's a slow-cooked stew and, sorry, you can't get it tonight. It's only served on Thursday and Friday. Most people buy it by the quart. It's actually not on the regular menu. However, I took the liberty of ordering dinner. A sampling of traditional dishes."

"Thanks, that sounds perfect," he said, leaning forward, his hand on his water glass. "I'm just sorry it has to be a short night. I've got this cocktail party to go to. It's a work thing. I'm up for a promotion at my firm, but since the last case was so successful, I've got some outside interest as well. So while it's called a cocktail party, it's actually an interview where you can get drunk during instead of after."

Although she was pleased his engagement at nine wasn't a date, she didn't want to show it. Instead she said, "I didn't realize you weren't happy at your firm."

"No, I am," he said. "But it would be dumb not to explore what's out there. The firm hosting tonight's affair has a very high success rate and impressive clients who bring in really challenging cases."

She chuckled, although she didn't envy him. "Wow. Big night."

"Yes."

"No wonder you look so dapper."

He rolled his eyes, but before he could comment, the kitchen door opened again and most of her family walked out, several of them carrying dishes. Zoya, who was nineteen, arrived at the table first with a bottle of the same red she'd brought them last time. "Be prepared," she whispered quickly to Natalie. "Mama mentioned your friend was a lawyer."

Natalie winced. As the juggernaut of Ukrainians approached, with murder in their eyes and their English, she touched the back of Max's hand. "I'm so sorry," she said. "At any moment, feel free to run."

His right eyebrow rose as the first plate, with three different kinds of pierogi, was placed on the table. The second dish was borscht, the third, kasha varnishkes, and the fourth, fish in aspic. Basically, a buffet of starters.

"You are attorney," Uncle Victor said, loud enough for the people across the street to hear. "I want to hire you to sue the pants off my thief of a cousin. Tonight!"

Max's other eyebrow rose, and the look he gave Natalie was mostly one of surprise, with a little panic mixed in.

# 9

MAX WASN'T SURE what to do. Natalie was into film—maybe this was some kind of cinema verité and there were hidden cameras behind the paintings. She'd warned him before that her family was nuts, but...

"I actually don't take personal cases," he said, but he didn't think anyone was listening. The other man, who looked a great deal like Natalie's uncle Victor, was promising to hire his own attorney, and saying that he would end up owning both restaurants. Victor would have to explain to his children why he had made them poor and homeless because he was a recipe thief.

Max leaned over the table, careful of his clothes. "I thought he was the brother-in-law."

"Also third cousin." She huffed an impatient sigh and said, "Oh, for heaven's sake," forcefully enough that the men shut their mouths. Boy, she looked great with that fire in her eyes. "I'm here with a guest and you're embarrassing me. I won't tell you twice." Her glare traveled from uncle to cousin to Aunt Hanna, then to several people in aprons. He knew some criminal lawyers who could take lessons.

The straight back, the determined expression and the commanding tone were having an effect on him, too. In a way that wasn't in the same zip code as the friend zone. As the staff retreated, the quiet was like a fresh breeze. Then his grumbling stomach made her smile and he could relax again.

He poured them each a hefty glass of Shiraz and started filling his plate with one of everything.

"I know," she said, lifting her wine. "They're lunatics. They're also wonderful, but mostly they're lunatics."

"The holidays must be interesting."

"You have no idea."

He lifted his own glass but he held off drinking as Natalie leaned in. "To be honest, I don't come here all that often. I think I scare them."

"Hell, you scared me. You probably didn't notice, but you could have heard a toothache in this place. Impressive."

She leaned back, took a sip and traded her glass for a fork. "Thank you. Now. Dinner. I'll explain the dishes, and we can enjoy what's left of our time together."

He began with the pierogi, which he'd had before, although these were much better. Or maybe it was the company that made them taste so good. She explained about the buckwheat groat that were at the heart of the kasha, and *varnishkes* turned out to be another word for bow-tie pasta.

Just as he'd dug in to the kasha, Ivan hurried out of the kitchen, checking behind him before he arrived at the table with two small bowls of condiments. "My idiot brother-in-law forgot these. And listen," he said, lowering his voice as he spoke directly to Max, "my cousin Joey just passed the bar with a very high mark. He's going to represent me in this lawsuit, so you might as well not take the case. It would be a waste of your time."

"Ivan." Natalie was getting that look again. He

held up both hands and backed away, and Max didn't blame him.

"My apologies," she said.

"Joey? That doesn't sound like a very Ukrainian name."

"When I said extended family, I meant it. I've got cousins and second cousins and cousins twice removed. Joey's one of the good ones, though. I hope he doesn't get caught up in all this mess."

"That's okay. It's interesting. The food is really good. Different, but good, and so is the atmosphere. My family isn't so extended. I have an aunt, Ellen—"

"You mentioned her before."

"Right. She's the one who wants me and my brother to be married. She has two kids, daughters. Around my age. We got in a lot of trouble during family gatherings, but that was mostly our fault, not the cousins'. We also have one grandpa who's still alive. He lives near my aunt Ellen in Vermont."

"That's it?"

"Yep."

"I bet they're all normal, huh? Don't yell across restaurants, don't throw entire turkeys at each other?"

He had to ask. "Cooked or raw?"

"Cooked. Stuffed. A twenty-seven-pound turkey. That was a very special Thanksgiving."

Max probably wouldn't have believed the story before he'd seen her family for himself. "I have nothing to top that. You win the weird-family award."

"Yeah," she said. "I get that a lot. Why do you think I got into films and books? I needed the escape."

He laughed. "Ah, it all begins to make sense. I grew up in middle-class suburbia. Mike and I were outside every minute we could be. We played all the sports, even the ones we were crap at. I wasn't much for reading anything but comic books until high school. Dawn Bryan was my high-school girlfriend for a couple of months in tenth grade and she was heavily into books. I thought she was sexy, and she thought I was a reader, and voilà," he said. "Magic. She had a habit of asking me about the books I'd supposedly read, so I read them."

"No CliffsNotes?"

He shook his head. "I never lost the desire to read, only the time necessary."

"That's a shame."

"Life won't always be this hectic."

They ate some more, and he found he liked the deep red borscht a lot. He liked her a lot. He wished she was going with him to the party. It would have made him more at ease. Not that he was worried. He just would've enjoyed having her there.

By the time he'd eaten enough to take off the edge, he started getting nervous again. His plan had worked, though. Natalie was a great distraction.

"It's almost time for you to leave, and we haven't talked about *M* at all."

A glance at his watch confirmed that the car would arrive in the next few minutes. "You're right. I wish we had longer." He folded his napkin and thought about finishing his second glass of wine, but passed. "We'll have to try again." He looked at her. "Don't get me wrong, I really enjoyed tonight, but I was serious about the movie. I'm very interested to hear your thoughts. My exposure to old films is limited, and I'd like to learn more now while I have the chance."

"You mean before you get this promotion?"

"Yep. Whether I stay where I am or go with another

firm, I'm going to be swallowed whole. No time for much fun at all."

"A promotion should be a reward. That doesn't sound like much of a win."

That stopped him for a moment. She had a point, but it was all leading to an endgame that was more important than time to relax was now. "Worth it, though." He checked his watch again. "You think we can find someone to give us the bill?"

"There won't be a bill tonight. Not after that nonsense at the table. If you haven't noticed, they're still going at it. I swear, it's like coming to the circus."

After putting a twenty on the table for Zoya, he stood and was about to say thanks again when the kitchen door swung open. It was Ivan tugging along a dark-haired guy Max hadn't seen before. The kid had curly hair, black-rimmed glasses and an attempt at a soul patch, and he looked as if he'd rather jump off the Brooklyn Bridge than be dragged into the dining room. Before they reached the table, a very unhappy-looking Victor made his own appearance.

Natalie stood up, tossed her napkin on the table and took Max by the hand. "We're leaving. Now."

Feeling like Clyde to Natalie's Bonnie, he hurried with her to the front door. When she stopped, it was to turn around, hold out her hand to the crowd still following them, and say, "I'm not kidding. Stop."

She didn't let go of him again until they were up the stairs and standing by the curb. With uncanny timing, the limousine sent by the recruiting agency pulled up in front of the loading zone. He opened the back door but kept his eyes on her. "Next time, we'll go somewhere else."

She glanced at the backseat of the limo, then back at him. "I—"

A half second later, he had his hand behind Natalie's neck and he was kissing away whatever she was about to say. The move surprised him, but not half as much as the fact that the impromptu kiss went from friendly to scorching in the space of a breath.

It was awkward with the door between them, with the car idling in the red zone, with the city buzzing around them. But it also filled him with the taste of her, the scent of her perfume and then the feel of her hand gripping his shoulder, holding him steady.

The sound of an obvious throat clearing brought him back down to earth. Natalie's eyes were as dark and wide as they could get, and he hadn't felt this flustered in years. He'd kissed her. He hadn't planned to, but he'd done it.

"Excuse me." A familiar woman's voice came from behind him. From the backseat. "Max? We don't want to be late."

Stella. She was supposed to be meeting him at Parlor.

"Sure," he murmured to her before turning back to Natalie. "We have to, uh…"

"Right," she said. "Okay. Um. Have a…good time?"

He nodded and leaned forward to say, "You still owe me a movie night," then slipped into the limo. Natalie closed the door after him. The limo surged forward into traffic before he could make sense of any of it. He watched her until a bus cut off the view.

"Well, that was a thick slice of awkward."

Max turned to his surprise companion. "I thought—"

"I know, I was supposed to meet you at the club, but I wanted the time to go over things with you. Now I'm glad I did. We need to get you focused."

"Yeah," he said. "No problem. Not at all. I'm completely here and ready."

Stella, who was not only beautiful but incredibly good at her job, didn't look convinced.

"Really. We're just friends. She knows a lot about old films. And Ukrainian food." He sounded lame, even to himself. Jesus. What the hell had he been thinking with that kiss?

"Max. You can think about her another time. Tonight's important. Other attorneys the partners are considering will be there, but you're going to be the main attraction. Everyone will be sizing you up. I swear, after all the work I put into getting you there, if you blow it, I may just kill you."

"Elliot Beckingham," Max said, blocking out any other thoughts. "He's looking for a shark, someone who can swim in deep water. He's got three major cases going right now, the most important being the pharmaceutical class action. Dan Grohl is the lead on that one, and I aced him out of the number-two spot at Northwestern."

Stella sighed. "Thank God. Now, let's go over your strategy. Particularly how you're going to handle the questions about you appearing in court more often."

"I know you like bringing this up, but they shouldn't be looking at me for my courtroom abilities. I'm there to make sure the attorneys who are in court have the best information possible."

"I keep bringing it up because you don't seem to believe me. They'll still want you to do that, but they'll need to know you're prepared to do the heavy lifting in front of a judge and jury. And that's not just Beckingham. All of them want the total package."

"Fine. Okay. I had more than my usual load of court

days on the seafood case, so there should be no problem. I'll still emphasize the research, though."

Stella smiled and pushed her long blond hair behind her shoulder. "As my father always said, lead with your strengths, but be ready for anything."

THE LIMO HAD disappeared awhile ago, but Natalie kept looking down the street. Everything around her had dulled to a muffle the moment Max had kissed her. Passionately. Sensually. There had been nothing casual about it. In no sense was it a friend saying thanks to another friend. Tongues had played a major role, and that didn't happen between pals.

*What the ever-loving hell?*

Unfortunately, she'd left her jacket and purse in the restaurant, but when she turned to go back, she found Zoya leaning against the stair railing, holding the items in her hand.

"I thought you said it wasn't a date," Zoya said.

"It wasn't."

"It sure looked like a date."

"You saw the…?" She waved vaguely behind her.

"Yeah. Me and the bombshell in the backseat."

Natalie inhaled and let out her breath slowly. "Yeah. That was weird, wasn't it? He said it was a business thing. I believe him. But I'm still very confused. I'm gonna go home now."

"Good idea." Her cousin handed over the jacket and purse. "You should avoid this place for a while. They're getting worse. I think they might actually go to court."

"Oh, for God's sake. Thanks for being one of the only people in this family who has a lick of sense. You should come over for game night soon."

"I will. I've got to go, but if you need to talk, I'll be home after closing." Zoya hurried back to the stairs.

Natalie walked. This time she'd worn comfortable shoes because she hadn't needed to dress up for a *friend*. But the kiss had blurred the edges between them. In a major way.

It wasn't fair. The conversation over dinner, despite the interruptions, had been interesting and so easy. They'd connected, and she felt certain that they could have talked into the wee hours of the morning. They'd each laid out clues, and she'd wanted to dig deeper.

Of course she'd been attracted to him, that was a given. Yet she'd been too engrossed to feel self-conscious about their sexual past or future. It was the kind of simpatico she hoped to find in a husband. Which was terrible. She'd had the best sex ever with a man who was fascinating and engaging, and who'd liked her enough to break their agreement never to meet again.

While a gorgeous woman waited for him in a black limo.

No, he'd told her the reception was business. She had no reason to believe he'd lied. After all, he didn't owe her an explanation about his love life. They were supposed to just be friends. Oh, God, she didn't need this roller coaster.

If she had a brain in her head, she'd cut her losses and move on. They hadn't even talked about films yet—Oh, no, wait, he said she owed him a movie night. If she followed through, she knew that was going to make things even more confusing.

The question was, could she do the smart thing? She'd have said yes if she hadn't gone into a frenzy when he'd showed up at work. The amount of money she'd spent on underwear made that achingly clear. Her judgment about these things had proven to be flawed.

If only she didn't like him so much.

If ever there was a scenario that guaranteed doom and heartbreak, seeing Max Dorset again nailed it.

THE COCKTAIL PARTY was at Parlor in SoHo. The club had such an exorbitant price tag for members that most people in the city couldn't even dream of belonging. Notorious for its privacy policies and its celebrities, it also made a statement about Beckingham & Quail. Elliot Beckingham was a sought-after fixer, rumored to have gotten some major players out of career-ending trouble.

The attorneys who worked there were definitely ruthless. Smart as hell, too. They made big money, but they dedicated more of their lives to the firm than even Max was comfortable with.

That didn't mean he wouldn't consider joining their team. This last case had proven he could be as ruthless as the best of them. After his talk with Stella, the thought bothered him more than it should have, though. Research was his specialty, he reminded himself, and he was persistent, painstaking and creative. If they seriously wanted him in the courtroom, they'd have to pay him a hell of a lot more for the privilege.

After passing the guest-list gauntlet, he walked into a black-and-white world. The space was huge, and the decor as moody as a Fritz Lang alley. Waiters carrying hors d'oeuvres and Champagne wandered through a very elegant crowd. He didn't recognize anyone, not yet.

While Stella went off to talk him up elsewhere, he made his way to the bar and ordered a glass of Shiraz. The cellars here were rated five stars, and he wasn't disappointed. He lingered, looking at the paparazzi photos blown up on the walls, the minimalist decor, which made the people the brightest things in the room.

Natalie would have liked this. The atmosphere felt charged, and if he wasn't mistaken, the negative-ion levels had been pumped up and the sound of conversations muted. Music played softly in the background. Bessie Smith.

"Mr. Dorset."

Max recognized the voice. Elliot Beckingham himself. The man was impeccably dressed. His signature white hair gleamed in the unique lighting, but his smile seemed too friendly to belong to a man with his reputation.

They shook hands while Beckingham gave him a once-over Max wouldn't soon forget.

"Rumor has it that Latham's win is covered in your fingerprints."

"Not completely. There were plenty of us on the case."

"There's no need to be modest in here, Max. You're familiar with our client list?"

"Of course."

"Tell me something," he said, looking suitably curious, though Max doubted the man ever asked a question without already knowing the answer. "This last case put you in the courtroom more than usual, didn't it?"

Nodding, Max kept his expression neutral. Stella had warned him, but he hadn't expected to get to this particular topic so soon.

"How did you feel about that?"

"I was fine with it. Although the partners came to feel I was more valuable researching precedents."

"I heard from a colleague that you did quite well in front of the judge."

"I'm not afraid of the courtroom, and I'm a reliable trial advocate. But I'm a firm believer in exploiting one's strengths. That case wasn't won in the courtroom, sir. It was my research that tipped the scales."

The man laughed. "All right. Excellent. A healthy ego is important in this business." He studied Max for another long moment. "I understand what you're saying. But we look for people who do well in many areas. The jury liked you. So did the judge. And meeting you, I can see why. You're a very engaging man."

Max smiled. Dammit, Stella had used that "total package" label the first day he'd met her. She'd been right to press him about it. There was no getting around the fact that he'd have to deal with the issue.

Beckingham put a beefy hand on Max's shoulder. "Make yourself comfortable. Mingle. Ask questions. Don't worry. Everyone who works for me will be straight with you. We expect a lot from our people. And the benefits are commensurate."

Max nodded. "I'll do that," he said. "I'll be sure not to hold back."

"Good man." After a friendly nod, Beckingham walked straight over to a great-looking woman in a killer black dress. Most likely to give her a similar spiel.

Except the woman was now looking at Max, so maybe she was already part of their team. Kind of young, under thirty, so she could be a second- or third-year associate. He wondered if she'd just been asked to keep an eye on him. Or to play escort. He wouldn't mind that. Information gathering could go both ways.

He glanced around and caught Stella watching him. Oh, she was good. He couldn't help but wonder if the two men she was chatting with were also her clients.

"Max Dorset?"

He turned to the blonde in the black dress. "Yes," he said, accepting her offered hand.

"I'm Heidi Dunn. A third-year with Beckingham & Quail. How about having a drink with me?"

Now came the part of the evening where he'd hear the firm's unbiased high praises, then find out what he could expect from "commensurate benefits" and a noteworthy wage. It might look like a party, but there was nothing festive going on.

"Sure," he said, smiling. "Lead the way."

With her big green eyes and mile-long legs, Heidi was a knockout. She'd be great company for a while.

He still wished Natalie had come with him.

# 10

A WHOLE WEDNESDAY off, and instead of reveling in crossing off items on her to-do list, Natalie was moping. She hadn't heard a word from Max since Monday and doubted she would. He'd probably kissed her out of some automatic reflex and had been kicking himself ever since.

Also, there was her mother.

God, the woman knew exactly which button to push to get under Natalie's skin. Last night was supposed to have been a nice dinner to play catch-up with each other. Solomon had cooked, which meant the food had been divine, but her mother had sipped too much wine and had plenty to say about Natalie breaking up with Oliver.

With her iced tea prepared, Natalie went back to her room to finish putting away her washed clothes. Her days off were supposed to be prime getting-stuff-done time, especially for a list maker like herself. Dry cleaning, grocery shopping, taking a box of clothes to the charity shop, researching a different ISP... The list was prodigious, but that was mostly because she didn't do idle very well. Reading and watching movies weren't being idle, but those were treats, after doing all the things. Sometimes when one of her days off fell on

Wednesdays, she went to a matinee at the theater. But that was out because she'd been a slug yesterday and hadn't accomplished anything. So today she was being punished.

She opened her underwear drawer and put away the hand-washed La Perla bra and thong she'd spent too much money on. She'd had Max Zimm's cell number since Monday. Had she called him? No. It wasn't because of his looks. He was…okay-looking. Dark hair, a little chubby, a nice smile. She'd have been happy to call him if she'd gotten his real card first. But she hadn't spoken to Mr. Zimm because she was an idiot. All she had to do was pick up the phone, go on a date and then, hopefully, she'd stop thinking about the other Max. It pissed her off that she kept expecting Max Dorset to call. She shouldn't have any expectations. They only caused her more grief.

With a sigh, she pushed the drawer back in, thinking about that singular moment when she'd first met him. And then, right after she'd discovered the printing mistake, she'd nearly made a clean getaway. But he'd touched her, and her life had been irrevocably ruined.

Okay, not ruined. At least not her whole life. Not even most of her life. But it still made her sad and confused. That curbside kiss kept grating against her like sand in an oyster, polishing a pearl of doubt.

Her spicy cold tea made things a tiny bit better. Cake would have helped, but she'd have to go grocery shopping for that to happen. And seriously, there was no excuse for her to buy a whole cake just because she'd been enigmatically kissed.

Her eyes closed as she remembered the way the noise of the city had faded to insignificance as he'd nudged her lips farther apart.

The doorbell made her jump and spill her tea. Probably someone selling something. Or a friend of Fred's. When it rang again, she made her way across the kitchen and down the stairs, getting ready to point out the no-soliciting sign she'd put up next to the doorbell where anyone with eyes could see it.

It was Max. Her Max. Standing on her doorstep, holding a bouquet of yellow carnations. He held them out to her like a kid offering an apple to a teacher. "In the language of flowers, these are supposed to say, 'forgive me,' but then I wasn't sure you'd know that, so I'm sorry I haven't been in touch since running off on Monday evening."

"I see," she said, although whoever told him about the language of flowers hadn't done their homework. Yellow carnations actually signified rejection, which she would never tell him, and how was she supposed to turn him away *now?* "I suppose I should put them in water."

He nodded, but hesitated until she said, "Well, come on in."

Making a sound that wasn't quite a throat clearing, he entered her home for the second time. Dressed casually in worn jeans and a tight-fitting gray T-shirt, he was clearly nervous. Upstairs in the kitchen, she reached for a vase in the cupboard above the fridge.

Max moved in close and easily beat her to the Wedgwood crystal that had belonged to her grandmother.

He handed it to her, along with a tentative grin. "I was going to tell you I hadn't called because it's been an insane couple days, which would be accurate but not very truthful. I know I left on a weird note."

She stepped over to the sink, where she'd be able to think more clearly and focus on the flowers, not the way his muscles bunched under that tee. "Weird is a good description. Especially since we'd originally agreed not to see each other again."

"You're right." His voice had lowered, which made the kitchen seem smaller and her heart beat faster. "I owe you an apology and an explanation, if you're willing to hear it."

The water rose as she held her answer, not 100 percent certain she wanted to pick up the dance where they'd left off. If the two days since that weird kiss had shown her anything, it was her vulnerability that was on the line when it came to Max. Despite their independent goals, their chemistry was volatile and could ignite at the smallest spark. It didn't help matters that he was maddeningly wonderful to talk to. Not daring to look at him, she put the vase on the counter and brought out her scissors to trim the stems. "The flowers already apologized," she said. "So why don't you stick to the explanation?"

"Okay. Good. Uh, you know most of it. Seeing *M* the other night honestly did spark my interest. I stopped by Omnibus on a whim, but I'd thought about pursuing something more with you." He spoke fast, as if he'd rehearsed the lines, but then he stopped. Cold.

The snick of the scissors was stupidly loud.

"A friendship. I mean, I hoped we could be friends, even though I wouldn't be a particularly good one, especially after I go back to work. But I like you. So I... went for it."

The flutter in her stomach had started when she'd opened the front door, but it had blossomed into something of an issue. She placed a stem in the water, then another. "I don't know about you, but I don't kiss my friends like...that."

His inhale was sharp behind her. It was tempting to turn around, but she held her ground.

"It wasn't part of the plan."

"I imagine not. Especially with your companion waiting right there."

"Shit," he mumbled and his sneaker squeaked on the linoleum. "I should probably have led with the fact that the woman in the car is an executive recruiter. I think I mentioned headhunters have been calling. Anyway, I've been working with Stella, but there is absolutely nothing going on between us."

Her sense of relief was immediate. She turned to find him standing close to her table, his fingers stuffed into his jeans pockets. "Either way, it's none of my business," she said, shrugging and looking away. "How did cocktails go?"

"Good, I think. It was flattering and nerve-racking. It felt as if everyone had been assigned a couple of questions so they could put all my answers together in some equation after I left."

"That sounds ominous."

"Not really. I think I was just nervous. I've been to parties like that, but I've never been the primary focus. Stella was there to make sure things went smoothly. She's very good, but I kept wishing—" He stopped. She didn't miss the look of alarm that crossed his face before he quickly neutralized it with a smile and an absent glance at the carnations.

Oh, she imagined he was a pretty damn good lawyer. She was curious about what he had been about to say and thought about waiting him out. But she took pity and asked, "Did you come away with any impressions of what it would be like to work for the firm?"

He shrugged. "Only that they'd want me to be in the

courtroom more than I've ever been, while still doing the research. Which would mean putting in more hours than ever. But they're a big firm and they get really meaty cases, and that's difficult to ignore."

"You like them tough, eh?"

"Oh, yeah. Tell me it's unwinnable, and I'm all over it."

"It sounds like there's a great deal to consider before you can make a decision."

"Building equity in my own future is my main motivation. But you're right. There are a number of factors involved. The firm's prestige, the methods for assigning work, the level of responsibility. This is just the beginning. It's sort of like rush week. I won't know what fraternity I'll end up with, but I want to visit as many as I reasonably can."

She realized she was smiling, and that her grin had nothing to do with the words he said. In fact, she dialed it down a notch because the topic of his future was serious. She just liked when he looked so relaxed. His hands weren't trapped anymore, his body language spoke of his easy confidence and he was somehow much nearer than he'd been a moment ago.

"What about you?" he asked. "You looked like you were ready to tear into me when you opened the door."

"I thought you were trying to sell me something. Actually, I kind of wanted to take on a salesman. I had dinner with my mother and her boyfriend last night. Normally, she's great, and I enjoy myself."

"But...?" Max asked.

Natalie turned away, picked up the filled vase and walked into her living room. Like all the other rooms, it wasn't large, but it did have the highest ceiling in the house, as well as a working fireplace. She put the flowers on the mantel, rearranging a couple of pictures and a pair of silver candleholders. "She's not pleased I broke up with my ex."

"Ex…boyfriend? Husband?"

Facing Max again, she wiped her hands on her jeans. "Boyfriend. She'd hoped for husband. I didn't dare tell her it was his proposal that made me end it. She'd have had a stroke."

He lost the smile and looked confused. Maybe she shouldn't have mentioned her ex. "I thought you wanted to get married?"

"Not to him. That would have been settling, and I simply won't do that again. Not where it counts."

Max glanced at his shoes, probably trying to hide his embarrassment. She hadn't meant to sound that sharp. He looked up again. "Now I get why you're so determined to get married."

"Because of my mom? No, it's not that. I want to get married for me, not her. As much as I love my work, I also want kids. And no offense, but I hate dating."

"None taken. For what it's worth, I'd never have guessed. You made the whole thing easy, even with the screwed-up trading card."

And there was the problem. For whatever reason, it was easy with Max. Irresistibly easy. "Can I get you something to drink? I'm afraid the cheesecake is long gone, but I've got some walnut bread that goes great with coffee."

"Thanks, but actually…" He closed one eye and tilted his head, looking at her intently for a long moment. When he straightened, he asked, "Do you have plans for the rest of the day?"

"Nothing impressive."

"How would you like to accompany me on a small adventure?"

She couldn't help the laugh that escaped. "What?"

"Seriously. I think you'd have a good time, and it would lift your mood. Mine, too."

"Where are you going?"

"I'll tell you if you insist, although it would be a better surprise." Closing the distance between them, he took hold of both her shoulders. "I promise, it'll be fun. Nothing fancy. You're already dressed for it. And it's not too far."

"That's crazy."

His eyes were particularly green against the gray of his shirt and the cream of her wall. "Yeah. But safe, too. Nothing that would make you uncomfortable."

The heat of his hands and the closeness of his body made her thoughts dart around like goldfish. She looked at his eager gaze, at the grin that she was already addicted to. "What the hell," she said. "Why not?"

"Excellent," he said, leaning in just before he let go of her and spun halfway around.

She wasn't convinced he'd meant to do that, but the offer of friendship was still the only one on the table. If she were smart, she'd let any other ideas go right now. Actually, if she were smart, she'd send Tall, Dark and Dangerous on his way.

"Maybe we could talk about *M* as we go? To Chelsea. We can catch a taxi on Houston."

"Will there be an opportunity to talk about the movie once we're at our mystery destination?"

He pursed his lips and looked up. "Not really."

"So, Chelsea by subway?"

There came the grin again. "Perfect."

THE SUBWAY LET them out about a block from his surprise location. There wasn't a way to make it appear from behind a cloak or anything, so Max decided he'd let the sounds give away the secret.

The ride over had been great. The city was as bustling as ever, considering it was a gorgeous spring day, but the bubble of conversation they created tamed the madness and wasn't difficult to maintain.

Natalie was exactly as he'd imagined, only better. She knew so much about Fritz Lang, the 1930s in film and political history, and the German influence on American directors. It was easy to ask questions, and she beamed when he asked something particularly astute. He hadn't felt that good since he'd gotten his scores on the LSAT.

He'd almost let it—having Natalie as a friend—drop. The day after the awkward kiss, he'd put off calling her because he hadn't known what to say. He still wasn't sure what had happened. It wasn't as if she was the only woman he'd ever have sex with again. Although, considering his date last night...

Gabbie had been as gorgeous as promised, but their night had limped along. She didn't want to eat more than a few pieces of sushi, and although she'd said she liked the Museum of Modern Art Russian exhibit, he'd caught her eyes wandering too many times to be an accident. Then she'd suggested a club, which was louder than hell and full of her friends, and by midnight he gave up trying. She'd walked him outside, and they'd parted amicably.

Paula wasn't even upset. She'd just said she'd keep working on it, and that was fine with Max.

But he didn't want to think about last night while he could watch Natalie fill in the blanks about where they were headed. The music from the carousel was the giveaway, and damned if he hadn't known she'd get a kick out of the middle-school carnival.

It wasn't very big. The length of two blocks, more or less, and the carousel music wasn't attached to an actual carousel. But there were booths with games and all kinds of artery-clogging food, a face-painting kiosk and kids by the dozens running amok down the closed-off street, among them Paula's two boys, aged seven and eight.

Natalie hadn't stopped grinning as they made their way through the considerable crowd. The perfect day—not too hot, cloudless blue sky—seemed to have brought out everyone in the neighborhood.

"How did you even know about this?" Natalie asked. "And how is this possible on a Wednesday?" They stood in front of a small roller coaster. There was one other ride behind it, a Whip-O-Whirl. Basically, a miniature ride fully contained on a portable stand.

"My cousin Paula helped put it together. Her two boys attend one of the private schools that are taking part. This week is the start of their summer break. They hold two events a year, this one and a Halloween festival."

"I haven't been to a carnival in years," she said. "I once won three goldfish throwing quarters into fish-bowls. Do they even do that anymore?"

He shrugged. "No idea. I let the boys lead me around until all my money's gone, and then they have no use for me."

"Sounds ideal, as long as you didn't bring the whole bankroll."

"I know better."

She surprised him by taking his hand and moved

them over to a milk-bottle toss, where the line was very long. The kid playing at the moment kept throwing the beanbag straight down in front of him. He got a stuffed mouse for his troubles.

"You might get lucky in this one," Natalie said.

"I wouldn't count on it. Now, if we were talking poker…"

She grinned at him, and he squeezed her hand. The surprise on her face made him sorry he'd reminded her of the innocent move, but she didn't pull away. "This is a very fine adventure," she said.

"I'm glad you like it. Silly as it is."

"Not silly. A side of you I didn't suspect."

He brushed a lock of hair that was teasingly close to her lips. "I told you I had a normal, boring family."

"Is your twin going to be here?"

"Nope," he said, unwilling to stop touching her. He traced the line of her cheekbone with his thumb.

Her eyes closed, and the cheek beneath him turned pink. This friendship thing was going to be harder than he'd thought. It confused him, this pull he felt. There was so much that appealed to him, but not in the way he was used to. Even if Gabbie and he had hit it off last night, he would never have brought her to meet Paula and the kids. He couldn't think of anyone else that he would have.

When her lips pressed together, he took the hint and they moved up the line. But when he was finished winning her a vibrant green plastic fish, he took her hand as he led her to the next booth and the next. Some were games, some sold kids' stuff. They explored, never moving too far apart, and in between the tents and booths, they would find each other's hands and as they walked, they bumped into each other way too many times.

She turned out to be really good at throwing darts. Just as she finished letting a little blonde girl pick a prize, Max heard a familiar voice.

"Max!"

Clay shouted once more before nearly toppling Max over, the seven-year-old barreling into his side.

"Whoa, cowboy, how much sugar have you had today?"

"Lots," Clay said, looking up from his stranglehold. "Mom says she's never taking us anywhere again. Ever."

"Max! Max! Look at what I won!"

There was Cory, running too fast for the crowd, a medium-size stuffed monkey waving wildly in his hand, hitting people every other step. Paula was running behind him, one hand gripping a big box of popcorn, the other a bobbing pair of helium balloons. Cory looked like he was having a ball. Paula, like she could use a drink.

Cory had to do some maneuvering, but he plowed into Max's other side without dislodging his brother. "See? It's a monkey."

"The best-looking blue monkey ever." He caught Natalie's eye, and she was laughing at him with real pleasure. Why the hell hadn't he called her sooner? At the very least, between all the work phone calls and meetings, they could have seen a movie or something.

"Oh, my God," Paula said, panting as she slowed. "You two monsters are grounded. Forever. I'm not kidding."

"Hey, Paula," Max said. "Looks like you guys are having a lot of fun."

"I'll show you fun, Max Dorset. You're babysitting. Tonight."

He laughed. "Dream on, kiddo. You've probably met Natalie Gellar from your dating group, right?"

Paula clearly hadn't seen Natalie standing just outside the very tight circle of boys. "We haven't met, actually," she said. "But I recognize you. I didn't realize Max was bringing a guest."

"It was a spur-of-the-moment thing. I was in a crabby mood. He figured this would cheer me up."

"Was he right?"

"Absolutely."

Paula grinned, still breathing a little hard. "I'm glad you're here. I'll warn you, though—I was going to sic these devils on him for a half hour or so."

"That's fine with me," she said. "Just give me a basic primer and I'm all yours."

Paula gave Max a look that said he could back out, if he did it quick. "We're old hands at this," he said, ignoring her offer. "We'll meet you at the corn dogs in thirty."

The other woman's look of gratitude was so great, Natalie laughed.

"You rock." Paula started backing up. "Don't give them any more food, no matter what they say." And then she disappeared behind a toy vendor's booth.

"Clay, Cory, I'd like you to meet my friend Natalie."

Clay let go of Max's leg and held out his hand. "Hi."

"Hi," she said, taking his hand. "It's nice to meet you."

"Are you good at winning things?"

"Not particularly," she said, stealing a glance at Max.

"Oh." Clay took his hand back. "That's okay. Max is good."

"So I've heard."

"I want to be a lion," Cory said. Then he roared. And roared, and kept on roaring all the way to the face-painting tent.

THE HALF HOUR with the boys was both hilarious and exhausting. Natalie was on prize-holding duty at the big-mouth clown while Max helped the boys try to get the bag in the hole.

She was in so much trouble.

It was her own fault, of course. Although she couldn't have known where this adventure would lead. Not that she'd have guessed that a school carnival could be such an incredibly romantic setting. Kids' games. Snow cones. Cheesy toys.

And Max. Touching her. Smiling. The desire in his eyes not fooling anyone. Of course she'd given up after five minutes at the carnival. After one last thought of walking away.

Now, as she watched him with the boys, who clearly adored him, she dug the hole she was in even deeper. All she could think of was what an amazing father he'd be. It was like watching her wildest dream come to life— and knowing she could get this close and no closer.

This wasn't so much a potential friendship as a guaranteed tragedy, but she couldn't gather the wherewithal to stop it. The feel of his touch had been so visceral, she'd found herself rubbing her own skin more than a few times.

Shuffling the monkey, mouse, plastic Coke-bottle glasses, striped fish and stuffed red owl in her arms, Natalie glanced at the corn-dog booth for the fourth time in the last ten minutes. There was still no sign of Paula. Today wasn't the day, but she'd sure like to hear what Paula had to say about her Trading Card experience.

Natalie had seen her at the meetings. Looks must run in the extended family, because Paula was very pretty, with layered dark hair, blue eyes and the same kind of tall, lean body that Max had.

The other Max, Max Zimm, was probably on a date right this second. With Natalie's luck, it was no doubt love at first sight. Maybe if she waited for five years or so, her Max would decide that having a family was more important than being a rich attorney and they could…

She rolled her eyes at her wishful thinking. She knew better than to believe that Max would be anything other than what he claimed to be. He'd spelled it out for her, and she wasn't deluded enough to think she could change him. A rich attorney with his looks? He could have anyone, and he was living in the land of plenty.

"What's wrong? You look like someone stole your lollipop."

She hadn't heard Max and the boys come up behind her, with Cory brandishing his brand-new rubber snake. "Nope. The lollipops are still in my back pocket."

"Well, something was wrong." He held each boy by the wrist, which was a good thing, because they tried to make a break for it every few seconds.

"Not at all. This has been the best afternoon. Really. I'm so glad we came."

The smile he gave her was equal parts proud of himself and not quite believing. "We'll send these two hooligans home soon, and then I'm taking you out for real food. No relatives allowed."

"That sounds nice."

He moved in a little closer, still wrangling the hyperactive kids. "Or maybe we could get some takeout and rent a movie. Another classic from the thirties? Go back to my place and you can do the live commentary.

I'll give you total control over the remote so you can pause to your heart's content."

"The devil you say," she said, thinking that sounded like heaven and hell wrapped with a bow.

"I'm glad I finally got my act together to come see you. I'm only sorry it took so long."

"I was thinking the same thing earlier."

"The only problem is—"

"Mom! Look at what I won!" Cory waved his snake as Paula joined them, looking refreshed. The boys were released and like wild condor chicks, they flew to their mother, who crouched down to hug them and listen avidly to their detailed reports.

Max started relieving Natalie of the toys in her arms. Paula handed him a big plastic bag she'd had in her purse and goodbyes and hugs were doled out generously. Natalie came away stickier, but happy to have gotten a peek into what a noncrazy family was like— and a bittersweet reminder of what could never be hers.

Max put his arm around her shoulders and pulled her in close. His warm gaze rested on her face and his cocky grin faded. "I have a proposal for you."

Her eyes widened.

"Wait." Max flushed and leaned back. "No, I said that wrong."

"Oh. I didn't think…" She started laughing; she couldn't help it. Even as his face reddened more, she couldn't seem to get control of herself. If she was clear on one thing, it was that Max wasn't asking her to marry him, and he never would.

Suddenly it seemed easier to sober up.

"I'm sorry. It's just—you should've seen your face." She drew in a quick breath. "Finish what you were about to say."

"Oh, shit." He still looked as if he might run after the boys. "This might be the wrong time."

"Please don't make me start laughing again."

He tightened his arm around her. "Would it be too much to ask that we maybe put off the friendship-only part of this friendship until...another time?"

She sighed. Then she rose up on her tiptoes and kissed him.

# *11*

MAX GLANCED BACK toward the stairs. "You're sure he's gone for the night?"

Natalie nodded as she put the smaller of two bags of Chinese food on her dining table. After debating the merits of restaurants on the Lower East Side, they'd decided to splurge on dumplings and other assorted dim sum from Chinatown. "Fred isn't coming back until Monday evening, so you can tap-dance to your heart's content."

"Uh, that would mean taking lessons, and I'm too excited about show-and-tell to do that."

"You've really never seen *The Lady Vanishes?*"

"Nope. But I have seen a bunch of other Hitchcock films."

"Did you know François Truffaut, who wrote an extraordinary book on the man, claimed this movie was his favorite and the best representation of Alfred Hitchcock's work?"

Max walked right up into her personal space and put his hands on her waist. "No, I didn't know that. Which is a perfect example of why I'm excited." The kiss that followed was slow and deep, and tasted like soy sauce from the dumplings they'd shared before they'd caught a cab home.

"I'm excited, too," she said, moving her nose to the other side of his before she continued what he'd begun.

The sounds they made gave her a thrill. Little moans and breaths and lip smacks and slick gasps. When his hands moved down to cup her butt, she wiggled against him and was immediately rewarded by the feeling of his erection pressing against her hip.

"We can reheat the dumplings later, if you want," she whispered, running her own hands down his back.

He groaned. "Once I get started, I'm not going to stop. So we should eat. Watch the lady vanish."

She leaned back. "That's probably a good idea. Tell you what—I'll point you to the trays and you can put the cartons on them. I'll be back in a flash."

"I'll miss you," he called out as she walked down the hallway.

Her grin was altogether too wide when she saw it in the bathroom mirror. There was absolutely no air of mystery about her.

The whole time she was washing up, she debated taking off her clothes. There were pros and cons, the worst of it being that she only had her schleppy robe in the bathroom. Her silky kimono was in her closet. He was busy with the food, so she could probably sneak in and grab it, then casually walk back into the kitchen all glamorous and stuff.

But then he'd be in his jeans and T-shirt, and she'd feel really, really naked. Not necessarily a bad thing, but how much actual movie would they watch? Did she even care?

In the end, she was too chicken to dare and she headed back to the kitchen wearing everything but her shoes. It didn't take them long to relocate to the bedroom, where they settled in to eat and watch the video.

"You really do have an impressive DVD collection," he said.

"Considering what I do for a living, I wouldn't be able to hold my head up if I didn't."

"Anyone who talked to you for five minutes wouldn't need proof of your expertise."

She started the movie. It had been simple enough to ignore the fact that the two of them were sitting so close that they kept bumping arms and elbows, and that the bed tray legs were poking into their thighs, but then she saw him purse his lips to suck up a long noodle. À la *Lady and the Tramp*. "This might just be my favorite thing," she said.

"The dumplings?"

She shook her head. "You and Hitchcock in bed, with sexy times for dessert."

The way he looked at her sent a frisson skittering down her back and she had to squeeze her legs tightly together. She thought she'd better turn her attention back to the movie before she completely lost it.

"There's very little music in this film," she told him. "See if you notice." He nodded, his gaze serious. But that was due to the spot of soy sauce he licked off the corner of her lips.

The dialogue began, and they were still kissing. Awkwardly. Not that she minded. Pulling back from his tasty mouth, she said, "The set the movie was shot on was only ninety feet long."

"Really?" He prepared a wonderful-looking veggie dumpling, but instead of eating it himself, he fed it to her. She tried to picture Oliver feeding her, and the image was so absurd, she choked.

"You okay?"

It took a minute until she could say yes. And now her

mascara was probably all over her lower lids. Wonderful. On the other hand, he was perfect.

The rest of the movie went by quickly, but by the end all of her attention was squarely on Max, and he'd pretty much stopped watching at all.

Natalie put down her chopsticks. He moved his tray and hers to the dresser. "Bathroom is down the hall, right?" he asked.

She nodded. "I'll meet you back here in a couple of minutes."

He kissed her as if they wouldn't see each other for a month.

She was weak-kneed and half in love.

BY THE TIME Max returned to the bedroom, Natalie had taken off her shirt. A red kimono painted with flowers lay across the comforter. He leaned against the door frame and took a minute. This day just kept getting better.

It'd started at the flower kiosk, where he had picked up the nice flowers. He still wanted to kick himself for not calling Natalie sooner.

She hadn't noticed him yet, and he watched her reach back to undo her bra. He thought about stepping in to help, but he was enjoying the show too much. He had an excellent side view of Natalie, and when the bra came off, the curve of her breast was enough to make his cock press against his zipper. Jesus, she was...lush. He doubted he'd ever used the word before, but then, he'd never seen Natalie exactly like this.

He'd better not get used to it. To her smile, her laugh, her shape. She was the type to see romance and sex as the same thing, and he had no desire to complicate her life. Or his.

He'd been up front with Natalie, though. She knew he wasn't ready to settle down. He just hoped when he went back to work, she wouldn't get too upset about his hours and his lack of attention. He'd make time for her, even if it was just a phone call. Now that they'd come this far, he didn't want to lose her.

"Are you just going to stand there, or are you going to take off your clothes?"

He jerked back. Her hands on her hips, she turned to face him, dressed in her jeans and not a lick more.

"I can be naked before you get those jeans halfway off."

Her left eyebrow rose while her eyes narrowed. "Deal." Then she was stripping down so fast he ripped his T-shirt and nearly fell flat on his face pushing off his jeans.

They tied.

But she was flushed and beautiful and that kimono stayed right on the bed when he pulled her into his arms for a very naked kiss.

For a long time, he just let his hands do what they wanted, which was everything. He cupped her breast so the hard nipple would rub against his palm, then he lifted it a little, frustrated that he couldn't kiss her lips and suck that nub at the same time. The nipple won out, and he bent to take it between his teeth. The sound of her sharp inhale only encouraged him more and he flicked the tip of his tongue fast, closing his eyes so he could hear every gasp she made. He didn't let up until her grip on his hair got a little too enthusiastic.

Of course, he couldn't just let her other nipple be ignored. It wouldn't be right, and he wasn't that kind of man.

This time, he used suction as his weapon, and somehow managed to get her all the way back until she had nowhere to go but the bed. He did let go as she fell back, but he recaptured his target in seconds.

She kept saying, "Oh, God." He wanted to hear his own name, but it would do for now. She'd cry out his name later, when he was driving her wild with more than his mouth. He knew it was narcissistic of him, but he didn't care. Listening to her gasps and moans made his cock pulse and his heart race.

He indulged himself for a few more minutes, and then he helped her move up the bed. They really should have pushed off the covers before they lay down, but he kicked and pushed at the sheets until he had a clear canvas.

Next to him, looking so sweet and pretty, Natalie giggled. He wasn't sure what she was laughing at when she looked at him, but he didn't want her to stop. Evidently, his expression got even funnier, because she laughed harder. So hard, she put her hands up to cover her face, while the rest of her—her breasts, in particular—jiggled along. A blush stained her neck and continued its path almost all the way to her collarbone, and it was impossible not to laugh with her.

He finally managed to say, "What's so funny?" but the words were garbled and somewhere in the middle of talking and laughing, he snorted. That set her off again, and she turned to her side, her back to him. She'd get it under control, only to burst out laughing a few seconds later.

Finally, the fit came stuttering to an end, with him spooned around her, holding her warm against his chest, listening to her smooth, even breaths in the pool of pale light from her bedside lamp.

"Can you talk yet?"

She inhaled loudly. "I think so."

"So what was so hilarious?"

Her sigh lasted until she'd turned around to face him. "I'm not even sure. I think it was mostly embarrassment, to be honest."

"Embarrassment? Why?"

"The covers. I hadn't realized you were going to kick them off the bed."

He pushed himself up on his elbow. "I should have asked. I had no idea it would make you uncom—"

"Stop," she said, holding him back before he could sit all the way up. "It's fine. I'm not used to it, that's all. Sometimes I laugh when I'm nervous."

"Natalie." He slipped down so they were eye level again and he cupped her cheek. "I can have those covers back up in two seconds."

"No, it's fine. Really. You've already seen me naked. I want to be comfortable this way. With you."

"Does it help that I think you look fantastic?" he asked as he sneaked his leg between hers, his arm around her waist. "That I want to touch you everywhere?"

"Yes, it does," she said, using her free hand to brush his arm from elbow to shoulder. "Looking at you helps a lot, too. Your eyes are mostly blue tonight. I love how they change."

"I imagine you won't see much but pupil soon." He shifted his hips forward, letting her feel how quickly his erection was rallying.

"Oh!" She reached down between them and gripped his cock. "I think I can help with that."

He moaned at the contact as her small hand slid from the base to crown. The way she touched him was exactly how he liked it. Firm enough to feel, but not without some room to grow. Her hips were moving, too, and he doubted she realized it. Soft pumps forward to match her pace. It was enough to drive a man crazy, and dammit, he didn't want to pop before she'd come at least once.

Before he could talk himself out of it, he stilled her hand and eased his way clear. She whimpered, and he kissed her. "Don't worry, we're just getting started."

He slipped away from her, off the bed. In two shakes, he had the sheet lifted so that she could grab it whenever she wanted, and tossed his condoms on the bedside table nearest him. Then he was on the bed again, gentling Natalie to her back as he covered her, careful to put his weight on his elbows and knees. "I've got too many things I want all at once," he said. "But the one that won't let me alone is to give you so much pleasure you can't remember your name."

"Wow. That's a really good goal. How can I help?"

He grinned. "Follow my lead," he said. "But don't be afraid to improvise."

NATALIE WAS PRETTY sure she wasn't going to make it through the night. She was trembling on the verge of her second orgasm, and with every thrust of his cock, his fingers found a new way to tease her clit until she was almost, *almost* there, and then he'd move them away as he pulled out.

His back was against her padded headboard, and she was basically sitting on his lap with her back to his chest. It was a position she'd never dreamed of, and she felt like some kind of exotic instrument that he was playing.

His strength was as much of a turn-on as his hands and his cock. He helped raise her hips up and down, which was a good thing, because on her own she would have been an uncoordinated mess. It was like something from a movie, from her wildest fantasies. He was lavishing her neck with kisses and licks and nibbles as his talented fingers made her gasp and beg. All the while, that big, hot erection was filling her over and over.

"You're amazing," he whispered, the heat of his breath tickling her ear. "I could do this all night."

She reached for him over her shoulder, placing her palm on the back of his moist neck. "Oh, God, Max. Please. Let me."

"Soon," he whispered. His teeth scraped the long tendon of her neck, making her shiver and whine. "Come on. You can do this. One more time. Up now, up."

She squeezed her inner muscles tightly around his crown, holding her breath, certain she couldn't make it last.

"That's it. Right there." He lowered her slowly as his index finger found the spot, the pressure, the perfect speed.

"Oh, God," she said, her head lolling back as the rest of her muscles tightened. One more second and she'd be there…

He filled her completely as she came, and it was as if her whole body was coming, from her toes to her eyebrows. She cried out and spasmed so hard she thought she might shatter into a million pieces. Nothing like this had ever happened to her and all she could think of was how was she going to give him up?

UNDERNEATH THE SHEET, Max had folded Natalie in his arms, their deep breaths almost synchronized. Part of him was still reeling after that last go-round. He'd always considered himself an adventurous lover, but she'd brought him to new heights.

Damn, just thinking about how he'd felt so much of her made his exhausted cock twitch. With her in his lap, molded against him, every moan had echoed in his own chest, every quiver and shift. He'd never realized how tight a woman could become in the moments before orgasm.

Hell, he'd come so hard he thought his head might explode.

There was no denying their chemistry together. No wonder he hadn't been able to let her go. It was different with Natalie. None of his ex-girlfriends had fit so well. Some had been amazing in bed, and great to talk to. Then there'd been Celia. They'd taken to each other in law school and started hanging out. She'd been so bright and so funny. But they'd never connected sexually.

Natalie hit every note. Almost.

And damned if that *almost* wasn't an insurmountable obstacle. No one would want to put up with his schedule once he started working again, not even if love were part of the package.

Boy, his hormones must've been doing a real number on him for him to be thinking about that at all. The only thing that counted now was that this arrangement worked for both of them. He'd talk to her in the morning. Ask her straight out if she would consider a friends-with-benefits situation. He'd hate it if she didn't want to sleep with him again, and he'd be deeply disappointed if she didn't want to be friends. But he'd deal. After all, his trading card was still out there, and, certainly, one-night stands were less complicated.

"Max?"

He'd thought she was sleeping. "Yeah?"

"I have to get up."

"Oh, no. That would be a real shame."

"I know. But I do."

"Anything I can help you with?"

"Don't think that's possible," she said, her voice husky with sleep.

"Oh. That kind of getting up."

She kissed his chest. Just a brush of her lips where he'd only felt her breath. It made him want to lock his arms around her and keep her there, close and safe. Instead, he rolled onto his back, freeing her, and brought up the covers to ward off the sudden chill.

He followed her progression from the bed as she made her way down the hall. Then he forced himself up, several of his muscles reminding him that he wasn't seventeen anymore. Or even twenty-five. The sex had been worth it, though.

He replaced the covers and set her robe back on top of the bed. Then he carried both trays and all the takeout containers to the kitchen, and put the ones that weren't empty in her fridge.

"Max?"

She must have returned to the bedroom. "I'll be right there." Before he left, he poured them each a glass of water.

"You prince," she said as he put one glass on her side of the bed. "You even took away the food."

"You sound shocked."

She had the covers up to her chest. Her bed head had been somewhat tamed, and he wished like hell his refractory period wasn't an issue, because he wanted her again. Now.

"I am," she said. "Although I shouldn't be. See what happens when you use the past to predict the future?"

He climbed under the covers and moved over until they were pressed together, his front to her side. "So what you're saying is, you thought I'd be like all the other guys you've been out with?"

"Precisely."

"Well, don't give me a pass yet. I'm still trying to impress you."

"You mean, at some point you'll stop?"

He looked at her, at her clever smile and her bedroom eyes. "I'd like to say no. But I confess, I probably will."

She turned until they were eye to eye. Close. "That's okay. It was very nice of you. Thoughtful."

He smiled and couldn't resist touching her face, the skin so soft and smooth. "I'm really glad I came over today."

"Me, too. It's been a great day."

His hand stilled and he moved back, taking a hold of the edge of the covers. "I should…go. I'm assuming that's what you'd prefer—"

"No, it's fine."

He threw the blankets back. "I don't want to put you in that position."

She leaned over and held on to his arm. "You can stay if you want to. I'd like it. But only if you want to."

The look she gave him seemed completely sincere. He was good at reading people, Natalie more than most. "I want to."

Her smile did more to convince him than anything she could have said. He did need to talk with her, ask her the hard questions, but not tonight.

# *12*

NATALIE WOKE TO the sound of Max snoring. It was a snuffle more than a freight train. That she found it endearing was worrisome. But then, everything about waking up to Max was worrisome.

Especially the fact that he made her so very happy.

He was strikingly handsome in repose. She'd thought it was his eyes that made his face, but she'd been wrong. They were gorgeous and unique, but his beauty came from his elegant bone structure. She'd toyed with the idea that this infatuation of hers was because of his looks, but rejected the notion quickly. The first thing that came to mind when she thought of Max was his smile, not because it was arresting but because it was so genuine. Because it made her joyful.

The last thing she remembered was snuggling against him, cradled in his arms. Sometime during the night they'd drifted apart, but not far. Her hand was on his arm. His knee pressed against her thigh. If she hadn't been afraid of waking him, she'd have stroked him, the dark hair soft on his muscled skin. He wasn't overly hairy. She'd rate him a five out of ten on a scale of hairiness. His hair was dark and it led to a defined treasure trail, which was a weird appellation, she thought, probably coined by a man.

Oliver hadn't been body conscious. Maybe because of the apron he wore every day at work. Maybe because he was too caught up in his fantasy sports teams to spend any time on his grooming. He didn't cut his hair until it got in his eyes, and then he went to the cheapest place he could find. His clothes were haphazard at best, and as for manscaping? That'd be the day.

Personal care said so much about the man. It made her think about what kind of a man she wanted to end up with. Max surprised her with his overt lack of vanity. Oliver had been far too content smelling of kosher dills. Reflections like this about real men, not movie stars, were as foreign to her as multiple orgasms had been before Max. But it was all good information. Information she filed under the heading Things for Which I Will No Longer Settle.

As much as she'd loved school, from kindergarten through graduating with her master's degree, this was by far the most exhilarating course she'd ever undertaken. The final would be brutal, though. Finding the man who would follow Max would be difficult.

Max snuffled, and his snuffle turned into a snort, followed quickly by a stretch. It dislodged her hand and his knee, but watching him squirm and wriggle was a treat. When he saw her, he smiled, then yawned, then smiled again. "How long have you been up?"

His scratchy voice would go into the archives to be replayed in the future when she was feeling stressed-out. "Not long. Haven't even brushed my teeth."

He didn't move in for a kiss, which was polite, although she wouldn't have minded. "You can go ahead and do that," he said. "I'll—"

"I have an unopened spare toothbrush. Minty-fresh breath for all. That's my motto."

He ran his hand down her back all the way to the edge of her butt, where he grabbed a handful. "I don't have to be anywhere at all today. No one's going to call. No one wants a meeting. And I'm in the mood for sex and deli."

"In that order?"

"Preferably."

She smiled. "You'll need to unhand me. Then I'll not only brush my teeth, I'll make coffee. Really, really good coffee that we can have before or after."

"How about before and after?"

"Done," she said, as she slipped out of bed and into her kimono. Much as she didn't want to rain on their parade, she had to go to work later. He'd obviously forgotten and she didn't have the heart to bring it up. She hated the thought herself.

After brushing her teeth, she grabbed a quick shower. She set out fresh towels for Max and called out, "Your turn," from the hallway, then went to the kitchen.

It was hard to believe how much she was looking forward to having more sex. This was unprecedented in her life. Sex before was like a corner-market cup of coffee in a disposable cup. Max was Kenya Kirinyaga Karimikui Peaberry, made in a French press and served at the perfect temperature.

She didn't have that particular blend on hand, but what she had was made to order by a local roaster, ideal for her equipment.

The pipes told her that he'd decided to shower, and she got out her glass canister of whole beans and measured out enough for two big mugs. The mugs were favorites of hers, from a local art fair. She even had fresh cream and natural sugar, which she put out in their own special ceramic set. It wasn't quite serving tea to the queen, but it made her feel good, and her coffee was a personal indulgence that made her days better. Very much like Max himself.

He walked into the kitchen without a stitch on. She grinned at his hair, which was damp and sticking out all over the place. "This isn't the first time you've talked about how good your coffee is," he said, walking up behind her and slipping his arms around her waist. "You've set the bar awfully high."

"I know it's indulgent. I pay a premium for the beans, but a great cup o' joe can make or break my morning."

"I can't wait," he said, bumping her butt with his burgeoning erection. "And I'm also looking forward to the coffee."

She turned in his arms and kissed him deeply as he groped her underneath her kimono. She considered skipping coffee for the bedroom, but no. She wanted this, not just to show off her amazing barista skills but because they hadn't slept all that long and she needed the caffeine. "I've got a terry-cloth robe, if you'd be more comfortable," she said.

"It's a little chilly, but I'm fine as long as I'm sharing your body heat."

Having no problem with that scenario, she got on with it. Boiling the exceptionally fine water, grinding, measuring and then pouring. A quick stir, and then kissing for three whole minutes.

Having him standing there buck naked was like getting a free pass to the best ride at Disneyland. Her hands traveled up and down and around and under him. What she liked best was the near squeak he made when she cupped his balls. Also, the fact that as it got harder, his penis sneaked between the flaps of her kimono all on its own.

The ding of the timer came too soon, but she didn't mind leaving him gasping behind her. Soon enough, they'd be alert and ready to do all manner of things.

She poured them each a mugful and he put a spoon of sugar in his. Then she waited, as if he were opening a birthday present. Of course he was going to say it was delicious anyway, but she knew his expression would tell the truth.

His eyebrows rose and his eyes filled with delight at the first sip. Ridiculously, she felt a huge rush of pride. It certainly didn't take much to make her day. A shared interest in films, especially old ones. Expertise in the sexual arts. An appreciation of good coffee…but mostly, she loved that he was honest at his core.

Yeah, she'd have no problem finding someone else like him.

"You make one hell of a good brew," he said. "I can't wait to thank you properly." He lifted his cup. "Can we take these into the boudoir?"

"I insist."

He kissed her, then got behind her again to follow her down the hall.

Three steps in, her doorbell rang. Natalie's happy bubble burst. "Oh, no."

"Fred's back?" Max asked.

She shook her head and shushed him with a finger to her lips. They both listened, and seconds later she heard voices. Which meant they were already inside and coming up the stairs. "It sounds like Uncle Victor and God only knows who else." She took his free hand and hurried him to her room. "I'll try to get rid of them, but it's not always easy."

He looked as disappointed as she felt. "Can you just not answer?"

"I would, but they have keys. For emergencies. They're coming up the stairs now. They have no personal boundaries. Usually, they at least call…" She groaned when she realized her mistake.

"What?"

"They probably did call but I turned off my cell at the carnival. No doubt I've got a half dozen messages."

"So they just come over if you don't call back?"

Natalie sighed. "Yes, if they think I'm depressed because you dumped me." She shrugged. "That night. We left abruptly… Maybe they thought… Never mind. I have to go deal with them."

Glancing at his rapidly drooping cock, he sighed. "I'll get dressed. Do you want me to hide in here?"

She thought about it as she grabbed her underwear from her top drawer. As much as she'd like to shoo them away, her relatives had no social skills to speak of and considered her home fair game. "No, somehow that'll just bite us in the butt." She dressed so hurriedly, she nearly tripped and fell as she pulled on her panties. "But they know I work today, so I should be able to get rid of them quickly."

He looked up from zipping his jeans. "Dammit, I forgot. I thought we had the day—"

She nodded. "I know. I didn't want to say anything earlier. But I can go in a little late." She put on her blue dress, the one that had the subtle flower pattern, and slipped into her comfy flats. Thank goodness she'd brushed her hair after her shower. "I'll meet you out there." With one last kiss before the swarm hit, she touched his cheek. "There aren't enough apologies in the world for my family, but I'm sorry, anyway."

"It's okay. Go."

MAX WATCHED HER leave as he finished dressing. Her family ruining their morning wasn't the worst thing in the world. That she had to go to work was higher up the list. So was the fact that he'd forgotten. He'd planned on taking her to breakfast and thought they'd go back to his place after. Now he felt like a dick for announcing he had nowhere to be today and was in the mood for sex and deli. As if the damn universe revolved around him.

He could make it up to her. But he wasn't sure how he was going to get through the next…however long it took her to get rid of her relatives. They certainly weren't quiet. He recognized Victor's voice coming from the living room and hoped Ivan wasn't there, too. So far, there hadn't been any yelling. That had to be a good sign.

He wasn't going out there without finishing his coffee, though. He had to admit it was damn good, but what he liked more was the way she was so into it. When Natalie felt passionate about something, she didn't hold back. Last night she'd been amazing. So enthusiastic and responsive it made him want to grab her and run.

Instead, he squared his shoulders and headed out to meet the family. Oh, man. There wouldn't be any doubt that he'd spent the night. Guess she wouldn't be able to pull off the "he's only a friend" deal anymore. And they'd know he definitely hadn't dumped her.

Her small galley kitchen was packed. Victor and Hanna were there, as were an older woman and a young man Max didn't recognize. Everyone but the young guy seemed to be talking, all at once, and a plate of blintzes was being uncovered. Then he was noticed and the chatter wound down as one person after another turned to stare at him.

"Yes," Natalie said. "It's Max."

Victor's mouth opened.

Natalie's hand went up in front of his face. "Don't even start. In fact, you should just put the foil back on the dish and take it with you. We have somewhere to be before I go to work."

"You didn't answer your phone," Hanna said, her voice accusing.

Natalie sighed and turned to the older woman Max had never seen before. "Hello, Aunt Luba. Good to see you," she said. Then she looked at the young guy. "What are you doing here, Joey?"

Max recognized the name as belonging to Natalie's recently graduated attorney cousin. Joey's eyebrows shot up for a second, then furrowed. "I should have known better. I was told you were expecting us."

"Oh, God," Natalie said, letting her head sag to her chest.

"What?" Hanna looked indignant. "You didn't answer any of our calls, so we come over. You could have been lying sick. Robbed. Who knows in this city?"

"This is insane. Joey, I'm sorry."

He glowered at Hanna. "They haven't stopped talking about this idiotic business since I saw you on Friday. Mom says I have to have a legitimate reason not to take the case because 'it's stupid' isn't good enough."

"Don't be disrespectful," Luba said.

At the same time, Victor said, "Hey, big-shot lawyer, you think you can speak to me like that? I'm still your elder, and your cousin, and you should show me respect."

"Why are you people discussing this?" Natalie said. "You and Ivan can disagree all you want, but when you start to bring in innocent people…" She shook her head. "I'm not getting involved. And neither is Max.

I mean it." She grabbed her French press and rinsed it out. "You know what? You can stay here, eat the blintzes. Just clean up after yourselves, and from now on, you have to wait forty-eight hours before you can barge into my home, whether you think I'm sick, depressed or if I eloped with the postman."

That caused another outburst, but Max was now inching his way to the front door. He found Joey was doing the same from the other direction. They met in the middle and shook hands. "Joey Balaban," he said. "Recently situated as temporary counsel at the Legal Aid Society."

"They do good work. Max Dorset, Latham, Kirkland and Jones."

"I've heard of them. Didn't they just win a huge ruling?"

The craziness in the kitchen had mostly died down, and Natalie had turned his way. She'd asked him before about his work, and he'd hesitated. Not that he was ashamed of what he did, it was just that most people wouldn't understand. Especially when the winning side was so unpopular. "Pretty big, yeah. So what's your specialty?"

"Criminal law, although I may need counsel of my own if my family doesn't stop with this absurd lawsuit. Sadly, I don't know that I'll have a choice, unless I can convince them to drop it. That's the main reason I came today. I know Natalie is the only rational one in the bunch that they actually listen to, and I figured the two of us would have a better shot at nipping this in the bud than just me."

"So the whole family's like this?"

"Oh, yeah. Every last one, including my grandfather who turns ninety-four this month."

"Amazing. On the plus side, you guys will never be lonely."

"True. And there's always lots of great food."

"Max?" Natalie approached. "You ready to go?"

"I am."

"You cannot be serious," Victor said, his voice louder and lower. "We came all the way over. The blintzes, they take me hours to make. By hand. With my own pot cheese, not what I use in the restaurant. Although the restaurant blintzes are plenty good. First place two years. *The New York Post!*"

"They look delicious," Max said, "but we were already on our way out. Perhaps another time?"

"Perhaps," Victor repeated, not very nicely. "Natalie. You call me when you're done with your very important appointment, okay?"

"Remember, I have to go to work." She took Max's hand. "And please stop harassing Joey. He's got his own life to worry about. If you're so desperate to work things out, get some boxing gloves and the last man standing wins." Before another word was spoken, she'd pulled Max out and they raced down the stairs.

Finally, they were on the street, and scurried like thieves around the corner. When the coast was clear, Natalie let his hand go as she stopped. "That went pretty well, I think."

"We made it out alive. And I really liked that bit about duking it out."

"I feel bad not taking Joey with us, but he's a bigshot attorney now. This is good practice."

Max grinned. "I've got to say, those blintzes did look great."

"Do you want to go back?" Her lips twitched. "We can do that."

"Uh, no." He laughed and grabbed her hand. "Any idea where we're headed?"

"None."

"We can always go to my place."

"You have coffee?"

He nodded. "Not as fancy as yours, though."

"We'll survive."

They started walking again, and it was nice, just holding hands and not being in any particular hurry. "We could go to Katz's Deli if you want."

"There's bound to be a huge line," she said, "but if you want, sure."

If it was going to be a choice between eating and going to his place... "What time do you have to be at work?"

Natalie's smile made it all the way to her gorgeous brown eyes. He doubted he had to verbalize his vote.

"Not for another hour and a half."

She leaned in to him to let a family walk by. The stroller had twins in it, and there were three other toddlers with them, all connected by leashes. "What made you decide your specialty? Tort law, right?"

He wished he'd steered the conversation to something else. "Basically. I specialize in civil law. Mostly because of the research. It's a little like being a detective. I search for the right precedent, the more obscure the better. I've even used ancient Greek references to make a point."

They'd slowed almost to a standstill. Her head was tilted up, and their eyes met for a few seconds. "If it's okay with you, I'd rather not talk about work. It's supposed to be my vacation and it seems I've had to be *on* too much lately."

"Of course," she said, but he caught a hint of worry

in her expression seconds before she broke out in a smile. "If I'm not mistaken, we're pretty close to your loft, right? Let's get moving."

He stepped up the pace, but his thoughts weren't so much on what they were about to do as what he'd just done. He'd dodged her questions again. He knew why. For the same reason he'd stayed off-line and away from newspapers for the past week.

In his world he was a hero, but he wasn't so self-centered that he didn't realize how most people viewed the victory. Natalie definitely fell in the most-people category, and he wasn't anxious to let her know he might actually be the villain.

# *13*

THE FOLLOWING MONDAY, Natalie arrived at Omnibus just in time. It had been a difficult morning. With Max in her bed, she'd been sorely tempted to play hooky, but then he'd have had to skip his meetings, which could mean the difference between a good position and a great one. So they'd showered separately, behaved like grown-ups and gone their separate ways.

The memory of him was still with her, though. The feel of his hands was like a map of her erogenous zones, some undiscovered until he'd touched her. She wondered if the sensation of lips nibbling on the inside of her wrist had always held the capacity to make her ache, or if her desire was triggered by his lips in particular?

While she was able to focus on her work for the most part, snapshots of moments she'd shared with Max kept sneaking to the fore. Good thing she didn't have to operate heavy machinery or she could have had a problem.

First up for her at work was a review of her upcoming article for the International Federation of Film Archives. But instead of going directly to her draft, she typed Max's name into the search engine on her computer.

She'd done a quick Google search after their first night together, but she hadn't gotten much farther than his Facebook bio. Everything there had been what she'd expected: his education, the firm he worked for, his serious lag in posting due to being so overworked.

This time, however, it wasn't Facebook she was interested in, but LinkedIn. And a quick glance at his profile told her what made him such a sought-after attorney.

His firm had won a hard-fought toxic tort case that could have cost its clients millions. Max was mentioned in two articles as being resourceful and dedicated. The partners took the lion's share of the credit, but anyone could read between the lines.

She didn't understand much about the case until she looked at some articles not written by and for attorneys. One, in particular, made the repercussions of Max's victory achingly clear.

The case truly was major, and the win had been completely unexpected. At issue were levels of mercury in commercially sold tuna, and the fact that there were no warnings that eating canned tuna more than a few times a week could be dangerous. Not because those suing the seafood industry didn't have a strong position, but because there was a legal precedent already in place that made it impossible to challenge the status quo without changing the way the U.S. Food and Drug Administration worked. Evidently if a product was regulated by a federal government, consumers weren't allowed to sue.

Natalie had had no idea that was the case, and while finding that precedent was very impressive, she wasn't all that thrilled with the idea as a result consumers could be at risk.

A gentle tap on her office door made her jump. "Come in," she said.

Her colleague Veda stepped inside. "Got a minute?"

"Sure." Natalie smiled and closed all her open tabs. Her stomach and chest were both tight, but she had to let her personal life go for now. She never should have looked him up at work, where she didn't have time to make sense of what she'd read. Veda sat in one of the guest chairs. She'd worn one of her more colorful outfits today, very demure and pretty like the woman herself. Her smile dimmed as she leaned forward. "Are you all right?"

"Yes. Fine. Thanks. Just going over my schedule for the day. What can I do for you?"

Veda hesitated long enough to signal she didn't believe things were fine at all, but she didn't push. "The folks starting the new film course at Yale can only make it here right after the Historic Preservation Symposium, so we're going to have to shuffle some things around. I was hoping you and Rick and Danny could work with me this afternoon so we could get the meeting schedules squared away."

"If we can do it between four and six, that would be great, because I have to teach a class after that and I won't be done until ten."

"Great." Veda didn't stand. "I don't want to intrude, but maybe you shouldn't be here at all today. I don't think I've ever seen you look so pale."

"It's nothing. Well, it's something, but it's not my health. I'm just confused. It's a guy problem, which is ridiculous. Especially with all we've got going on here."

"Did something happen with you and Oliver?"

Oliver? Right. She hadn't told anyone. "We broke up, but that was my choice and I've got no regrets." Natalie could hardly believe she was even talking about this at work. Although Veda was nice, they didn't connect that way. But now that the door was open…

"I've got some time now if you want to talk."

Before she could stop herself, Natalie said, "I don't

even know the whole story yet. I've been seeing this man. He's more of a friend than anything else because we don't want the same things. But I've just learned something about him that upsets me. It shouldn't. I mean, I'm sure he was just doing his job, but I'd imagined him being...better."

"He's someone new in your life?"

She nodded. "We met by accident, but he's funny and smart and he's honestly interested in film...and me. He doesn't even mind my crazy relatives, which is something, trust me."

"Sounds to me like you two are still in the honeymoon phase..."

"Oh, no. He doesn't want anything more than a friendship, and I'm looking for someone completely different. Well, mostly different. Someone who wants to get married and start a family, so—"

"I just meant that you're in that new space where you're excited to be together and you can talk for hours and everything's shiny and thrilling?"

"Of course." Natalie felt her face heat. Not only had she crossed the professional lines she'd established, she wasn't even listening properly. Or making any sense. "He's very different from anyone I've ever known before."

Veda smiled at her, but it was gentle, not mocking. "I've been there. I met him in London when I was at university there. A gorgeous guy with an Irish brogue so thick and smooth you could spread it like butter. I'd only known him for two weeks before I was convinced we would be together forever. We couldn't get enough of each other. I thought he hung the stars. Then his wife came to visit."

"Oh, God." Natalie sat back in her chair. "You're

right. I've made Max impossibly perfect, haven't I? Now that I've seen something that doesn't fit, I'm blowing it all out of proportion."

"Maybe. Or maybe there's something you need to discuss with him. But your reaction, given the timing, sounds pretty normal. Sad, because it's not fun when the illusion is spoiled. Especially for us, right? We, who are so in love with the magic of film. I used to wonder if Gregory Peck had ruined me for all other men."

Natalie smiled. "You don't anymore?"

"Nope. I've got my William, and while he's not Atticus Finch, he's pretty great, warts and all."

The tension in Natalie's chest had eased enough for her to breathe again. She didn't have the whole story, and wouldn't understand it until she'd talked to Max. She needed to be able to see him as a real person, not this wonderful, magical being she'd made him into. He'd charmed her, and she'd let him. The ride so far had been spectacular, but if they were going to be friends now, they'd have to come back to earth.

"Thank you." Natalie walked around her desk and gave Veda a one-armed hug, which was right at the edge of her comfort zone. But in a way, Natalie had changed a little bit. Because of Max.

THE FIRST THING he did when he finally got home was take off his tie. Why had he chosen a profession where a suit was required every damn day? He'd amassed a two-week collection of really good suits, which was another reason he only had a couch and a TV set in his living room.

Today's meetings had been intense but worth it. He'd gone solo, but he'd spoken to Stella on his way back from seeing Thomas Hornstratter, a hell of an attorney who worked in international law. He'd been interested in Max, and wanted to know if he'd be willing to go in a different direction. It sounded appealing, just for the challenge of it, but it wasn't the best use of his skills. Max wanted to capitalize on his success now, when the iron was hot. There would always be big tort cases, and making a name for himself as the go-to guy at Horn-stratter's firm would mean a lifetime of security.

The downside was the hours, of course, and the fact that he'd be in no position to have a say in the cases. He hadn't thought much about it a week ago, but he'd been doing a lot of thinking about that particular snag lately. He'd stripped down to his shorts by the time he got to the bathroom. He shed those, too, and climbed into the shower. The hot water beat down on his back as he breathed in the steam.

He thought about the lunch he'd had near the Flat-iron building. The senior partner hadn't been there, but Lawrence Johnson was more of a figurehead, so it didn't really matter. His grandson, Peter, however, had been pretty persuasive. They weren't a huge firm, but they had a strong reputation as fixers. They charged outra-geous sums for stepping in when all seemed lost.

The up-front money wasn't nearly as good as some of the other offers coming his way, but the potential for making a killing was there. Unfortunately, he didn't care for Peter Johnson. He'd been a jerk with the wait-ers at the restaurant, and again with his driver. Men like that weren't uncommon, but that didn't make it easier to be around them.

He wished he could talk it over with Natalie. But she was busy tonight. After her regular hours, she had a special screening, so she wouldn't get home until after eleven. And then there was the fact that he hadn't told her enough about his work situation for her to even have an opinion.

God, how had he become such a coward?

Someone who *would* be home in about an hour was his dad. He'd call in forty-five, after he grabbed something from the bodega, so he could talk to his mom for a bit first. She hadn't been around when he'd called two weeks ago. He'd ask her about her friends and her scrapbooks and just enjoy how each bit of news would begin with, "Oh, oh!"

It didn't take him long to dress and head down to the local store. They had decent curry and a good salad selection, so he fixed himself two plastic containers, got a half pint of Chunky Monkey ice cream and a cold six-pack. Upstairs, he caught up on the weekend sports, modified his calendar, ate enough, drank a beer and then turned on the closed captioning, adjusted the sofa pillow and dialed home.

Sure enough, his mom answered, and it was a good talk. He considered telling her about Natalie, but she'd get the wrong impression. His vacation was coming to an end sooner than he liked, and before long, whatever he decided, he'd be back to the grind. There were two major meetings still to come: the yacht party hosted by the firm most likely to give him the package he wanted, and the sit-down with Kirkland and Jones, the two partners in charge of the staff at his current firm.

Although the offers he'd received thus far ranged from good to great, there were a couple of things no one could give him except for his home team. He knew the players there, he liked most of them and he'd already proven himself. Would more money and better perks be worth giving that up?

His dad picked up the second line, and Max took a

moment to say goodbye to his mom. Before he'd even finished, his dad stopped him. "Something's up. Want to tell me what?"

"Just trying to figure out my next move. A lot of people are interested in me now and I don't want to blow it."

"What makes you think you could blow it?"

"Come on. You know how competitive it is out here. These are shark-infested waters, and I have to learn to swim real fast. Finding the federal regulations precedent to stop the suit was a fluke. I'm not going to be able to pull a rabbit out of my hat every time."

"I don't know exactly how you found that connection, but I do know how you think. You've always been meticulous in your approach to a problem. Whether it's figuring out how to keep your brother from taking your new shirts or tracking down unlikely legal precedents, it's that kind of thinking that these people are interested in, and there's no way you're going to lose that no matter where you end up."

This was why Max was a damn fool for not keeping in steady touch with home. Well, that and the fact that he'd always had a good relationship with his parents and he didn't want to risk losing their closeness. His father had always been his chief adviser, the one he looked up to most. "Yeah, you're right. At least you are about most firms. Some, I think, do expect miracles."

"Then maybe you ought to cross those off your list. That's a lot of pressure day-to-day, son."

"The more they expect, the more they pay."

His dad was silent long enough for Max to get to the fridge. "I've never known you to be motivated by money. Tell me how it's going to help if you stress yourself into a stroke."

He brought another beer with him to the couch. "I'm only thirty. Don't bury me yet."

"Thirty will become fifty before you can blink. Trust me on this. Especially if you're working eighty- to a-hundred-hour weeks."

He'd thought about that from time to time. Mostly when he was with Natalie. "I met someone," he said, not quite sure why.

"Yeah?"

"She's a film archivist. Loves old movies. Knows everything about them, too."

"Well, this is different. You think she might be someone for the long haul?"

"No. Not for me, at least. She's a...friend. I probably won't see her much when I'm back at the job."

"That's a shame. Your voice changed when you talked about her."

"Yeah?"

"Yep."

"I haven't told her about the tort case. I've been seeing her for a couple weeks. And I've avoided her questions."

His dad was quiet again. Max took a big gulp of beer.

"Why do you think that is?"

"I wasn't the one in the white hat, Dad." He sighed. "I didn't want her to think less of me."

"Max Dorset, I'm surprised at you. Your job was to do everything within the law for the party you were representing. The verdict was never in your hands. It will never be in your hands. That's not the way our legal system works. Sometimes the outcome might not be what you want it to, but you were every bit the man I'm proud of in carrying out your duties. No one could have done a better job than you, and of that I have no doubt. Whoever hires you, they'll never have reason to regret it. They'll be able to count on you, which is not something I think those big New York law firms can say very often."

Max let out a breath and just held the space for a minute. He hadn't even realized how badly he'd needed to keep hearing that his father was proud of him. And he'd made a good point. Everyone in the system deserved the best representation possible. The process didn't always work for the good of the people, but he'd known that going in.

He just hoped that occasionally he'd be on the white-hat side of things. And he wished he had a few of those victories under his belt now. "Thanks, Dad."

"Don't forget that you have lots of options. Practicing a different kind of law. Opening your own storefront. I'm not saying you can't be with the big fish, Max, because we both know that's not true, but consider the life you want, not just the job."

Max knew what his father was saying, but the time to make his big move was now. Who was to say he would ever get an opportunity like this again? "I won't make my final decision without giving it a great deal of thought. I promise."

"Good to hear. You been talking to your brother?"

"Not as often as I should."

"Well? I'm pretty sure he's still awake. Why don't you call him, make it a home run instead of a double?"

Max needed the chuckle. His dad had always been bad at sports analogies. "I think I will."

"Take care of yourself. Remember when you're talking to Mike that your mother expects us to have dinner as a family before you get swallowed up by work again. And call if you want to hash things out some more. I've got to go take care of the darned leaky pipe under the sink, or your mother's going to skin me."

Max said goodbye, finished his beer and dialed his brother's number.

## 14

TUESDAY GAME NIGHT at her place had seemed like the perfect way to shift things from incendiary to cozy. Now that Natalie had had time to think about Max's job and what it meant, she'd come to a few realizations. One of them was that he was already a friend. She hoped it would last, but that would only have a chance if she stopped expecting him to be perfect—and if they expanded their relationship beyond sex and talk of films. This evening was a step in that direction. Especially because he hadn't been thrilled with the idea, but he'd been happy to spend time with her no matter the circumstances.

Max had been the first to show up at her place. They'd had a brief but intense make-out session, then cooled down when Fred and Tony had arrived, but that didn't mean the rest of the evening hadn't been interesting.

Max didn't look at the Scrabble board in the traditional way. His highest scores were gained by the clever use of suffixes. Some that completely changed the meaning of the original word. Which didn't please Fred at all. Her wonderful tenant was fiercely competitive when it came to the game, and he hadn't counted on losing.

Tony, Fred's date, had been an excellent fourth. He taught chemistry at a midtown high school. Even before Fred and Tony had become lovers, Tony had joined them for game night several times. His focus was more on the conversation than accumulating points. "So tell me something I don't know about you, Natalie," he said as he proceeded to clean up the game board.

"Okay," she said, guiding Max to the couch. "You know I grew up in the Bowery, and I worked at the Bowery Ballroom as a bartender all through college. It was good. Mostly I liked the music, but it didn't do my hearing any favors. Those bands are loud."

Max seemed stunned at the revelation, although she had no idea why.

"What?" She frowned at his odd look. "It was down the block from my house. I needed a job that left me free for classes."

"I figured you'd worked in a library," he said. "Actually, I can't imagine you anywhere but at Omnibus."

They were sitting close together, his arm around her shoulder, her legs curled up beside her. She tugged his hair. "Hey. I have hidden depths."

He smiled as he studied her. "You certainly do. I imagine it will take me a long time to uncover them all."

The words alone were enough to send her heart racing, but she curbed her enthusiasm because she'd promised Fred there'd be no flirting, and definitely no hanky-panky while they were all together. "Your turn, Max," she said. "Tell us something surprising. And deep. Don't skimp on the deep."

"Wait a minute." Max reared back to give her a long look. "Deep? Working as a bartender isn't deep. Now, if you'd run off to Russia with a bass player and lived off vodka and starry nights, *that* would be deep."

She blinked at him. "Vodka and starry nights? Impressive. Go ahead," she said. "Show us how it's done."

"When am I going to learn to keep my mouth shut?" His eyes narrowed as he thought. Then his gaze drifted a bit and she could tell he was seriously thinking about what to say. "When we were little, my twin brother Mike was hit by a car. We were seven, and it was bad. I have very spotty memories, but mostly I remember being terrified that I'd done something wrong. I hadn't even been outside when he was hurt, but my parents were so scared it rubbed off on me."

Natalie curled her fingers in between his. It twisted something inside her to hear his story. He'd jumped into the deep end, all right. The mood in the room had changed. Fred and Tony had grown still at the folding table they'd played on and no one was touching the excellent scotch that Tony had brought.

"Mike and I were comic book freaks." Max smiled as if he were halfway back to age seven. "We came by it honestly, though, because my dad was a collector. We'd grown up on superheroes. I was Superman and Mike was Batman, and not only on Halloween. On the day of Mike's surgery, I put on my costume and put Mike's into his backpack and I told my dad that we needed to go to the hospital and make sure Mike was Batman so that he'd be okay."

The image was so clear, Natalie's heart melted. "Oh, God, that's the sweetest thing ever."

Fred rolled his eyes at the same time he nodded, and Tony leaned his shoulder against his boyfriend's.

"Dad told me Mike couldn't wear his costume at the hospital, and I got really upset. So *he* put on Mike's black cape, his tool belt and a Batman mask he'd worn the year before to take us trick-or-treating. We went to the hospital like that. Sat in the waiting room for hours as he read me one comic after another. Mike got through the surgery just fine. He's got a couple of hefty scars and he limps when he's overtired, but altogether, he got lucky."

"That right there is one hell of a dad," Fred said.

Natalie nodded. She wanted to be closer to Max, but they were already pressed against each other. "What an amazing memory. And your dad, what a great role model."

"Yeah, he was. Is. He's still the person I go to for advice when things get hard."

"My father was not a hero of any kind," Fred said. "In fact, we haven't spoken since I was seventeen, and I don't intend to change that. Ever."

"Oh, man." Tony frowned. "I had it easy with my pop. He died a couple of years ago, but he was cool with who I am. I mean, he didn't freak out or anything when he found out I wanted to be a chemistry teacher."

The laughter felt good. The whole evening had. She'd been worried that she'd feel differently about Max since reading about the tort case, but there was so much to honestly like about the man that she couldn't see making a big deal out of his work decisions. She wasn't even sure she wanted to bring it up anymore.

His story had been gorgeous. Just the thought that he'd chosen that to share showed her so much about what a fine, secure man he was. Any friendship with him would be richly rewarding. But also very difficult. Tonight had just reinforced the fact that he was exactly the kind of man she wanted as the father of her children.

Maybe the whole problem would be solved when they were forced to be apart more, after he went back to work. She'd have time to get over this little honeymoon of theirs and get serious about a realistic man to date.

"What's your dad like, Natalie?" Tony went to the mantel where he'd put the scotch and poured for himself and Fred. She passed, and so did Max.

"He was nice, although I didn't know him well. Very obsessed with his music. He was a professional cellist, and he spent a great deal of time playing. And he was older. Forty-seven when they had me. Honestly, he wasn't around a lot. My mother basically raised me."

"I'm sorry about that," Max said. "I was lucky."

Natalie rested her head against his shoulder and closed her eyes, basking in the closeness of their bodies, of the strength of his arm around her. But it was late, and the mess from the evening had to be put to rights.

Somehow it ended up being Max and Tony who tackled the folding table and chairs while Fred grabbed the last of the dishes and met Natalie in the kitchen, where she was already running the hot water in the sink.

"I swear," Fred said, keeping his voice low, "that story about the costumes nearly killed me. I love that he talks about his family like that."

"Tony's great, too."

"Yeah, he is. I like him a lot. But Max? So far I've been impressed with everything I've seen. He's special, kiddo. And you know I don't say that easily."

She busied herself scrubbing a dessert plate. "He's not as perfect as all that," she said. "But that's okay, because being with someone perfect would get real old, real quick. Besides, the deal hasn't changed. Once he's back to being Super Attorney, I'll be lucky if I see him once every couple of months."

"I don't think so. I think that excuse was him hedging his bet before he knew you."

"Nope." She put the last of the plates in the drainer. "He really is going to be swallowed by his work. This has been more like a vacation fling than anything else. And he's given me something to shoot for that isn't simply 'better than Oliver.'"

"Good luck with that." Fred picked up a dish towel, and then put it back down. "Oh, God. I'm sorry. I didn't mean—"

"Yes, you did. It's not as if I haven't already realized how screwed I am. Still, there's always hope."

"Of course there is," he said, although the look on his face certainly didn't show it. "Hey, if he's done nothing else, I know he's changed how you feel about yourself, and that's worth a hell of a lot."

"That's true. I am more confident. And I have better underwear."

Fred fist-bumped her as they were joined by Tony and Max. "As I was saying," Fred said archly, "I really hate that your boyfriend won, because I'm supposed to be the king of Scrabble, but I'll do my best to recover my pride and move on." He faced the winner with narrowed eyes. "Next time we're playing Dungeons & Dragons, and I'd like to see you win that one, Mr. Triple Word Score."

Max laughed. It was nice. The goodbyes continued as they walked to the door. Once it was closed and locked, Max pushed her back against the wood and kissed her. It made her blood heat and stilled her mind until there was only one place she wanted to be.

There were dishes to be put away, but she ignored them. Dropping clothes like breadcrumbs, they kissed the whole way down the hall and by the time they were between the sheets, there was no part of her that wasn't ready. She didn't want to waste a minute.

Six-thirty should have been too damn early to feel this good, but Max had two fingers inside Natalie, who was straddling him, even though she was barely awake. Her head was resting on his chest, and her mix of sleepy, slow and mussed up made everything right with the world.

"What are we doing?" she asked, her words slurred and her hand flailing at her hair, only for her curls to win again as she moved her hips so his fingers could go deeper. She wasn't doing a very good job of it. Mostly letting him do all the work, but that was fine. Better than fine.

"We're waking up," he said. "With sex. And for the record, you climbed on top of me."

"Ah," she said as she closed her eyes. "I'm very clever. This feels wonderful."

"I know. Wait till it's more than fingers."

"What?"

"Nothing."

"Okay. Oh!"

Because sometimes he was a freaking genius, he'd already taken a condom out of the packet. Unfortunately, he had to help Natalie sit up on her own in order to put the damn thing on. "Can you stay like that?"

"All right," she said.

He let go.

She fell forward just enough to block any possibility of him reaching his cock.

He tried again. This time letting go of her at a different angle, and waiting to see if it was going to be possible at all.

Instead of trying to manage her hair, she anchored herself with a hand on his chest. He was able to slip underneath her and sheath himself. "Done," he said.

"Wait. Already?"

"Not done with sex. Done with…it doesn't matter. Maybe I should just let you sleep a little longer."

"No. Don't do that." She wiggled her butt. "I like you a lot better than my alarm clock."

A little shift of his hips, a hand to keep her steady, and there he was in position. He took his time entering her, and when she squeezed him and moaned, the world became better than ever.

"Max. Max. Wait."

He froze. "Is something wrong?"

"No. I need to—" She flipped her head back, and finally he could see her beautiful face, her half-lidded eyes and the flush across her cheeks. "There we go," she said. "Carry on."

He laughed, and they both jiggled, but then he pushed in and she tightened her muscles and there was no room for anything else as the hot wet heat of her surrounded him, and she sat up and arched her back.

Last night after they'd hit the sheets had been fast and furious and hotter than hell. They'd attacked each other like heathens. He'd thrown her legs over his shoulders and if the guys downstairs hadn't heard them, then they weren't trying, because she'd been loud.

Now it was all slow motion and small movements. The way her upper teeth gripped her lower lip, making it pale until she opened her mouth. Watching her lip plump back to pink was maddeningly erotic.

Her nipples were stiff and puckered, and the temptation to suck them was agony. But he held off in order to take in the stretch of her neck, the flush spreading across her chest. The flutter of her tummy, and the low groan when he finally bottomed out.

"Faster," she said, adjusting her knees until she could

balance without touching him. Her index finger moved in a straight line down from her sternum, past her belly button, to her clit. "More," she whispered, touching herself.

God knew he tried to hold out, but watching her... He finished before she did. Thankfully, not by much.

After she finished coming, she flopped down next to him as though someone had cut her strings. They lay beside each other, panting, too wasted to move, even though he wanted to look at her.

"Natalie."

"What?"

"Is today one of your days off?"

She moaned as she smooshed her face against his arm. "We could have slept in."

"Are you sorry we didn't?"

She raised herself up just enough that he could see her smile. "Nope."

He turned more onto his side. "Friday night," he said. "Come with me."

"Huh?"

"There's a party. On a yacht moored at Chelsea Pier. It's kind of dressy and there'll be cocktails and a lot of lawyers. Come with me."

"That's an interview. You'll be working."

"Yes and no. It's not really an interview, not in the traditional sense. I've wanted you to come before, but this one will be nicer. The yacht's big. There'll be a live band. I'll have to leave you a little bit, but not for long."

"I'll be a distraction."

This time she sat all the way up and by the look she gave him, she was wide-awake.

"I'd like you to come. But whatever you decide is fine."

"Where is this yacht going?"

"Nowhere. That means if it's awful, you can sneak off and no one'll be the wiser."

"Can I let you know when I'm not chock-full of sex hormones?"

"Spoilsport. Of course you can."

"Tentatively, yes, then," she said.

He grinned. "Tentatively, yay."

She kissed him and flopped down on her back. "I read about your case," she said, staring up at the ceiling. "It was a major deal. I can see why they all want you to come work for them."

He felt as if he'd been sucker punched. His gut tightened and his heart, which had just gotten back to normal, raced into fourth gear. "I was going to tell you," he said. "But I wasn't sure how you'd react."

"I gathered. I'd like to understand more about what you did. From the articles, it seemed to me that you capitalized on an iffy stance from the FDA?"

"That's about right. I brought it to my boss's attention." He was playing down his role. Not intentionally, but Max heard it in his voice. He wondered if she could hear it, as well. "It turned out to be important."

"I also read that because of the final ruling, there are lawsuits coming up to challenge the FDA's position."

"That's true, too."

She sat up again, cross-legged, the sheets pooling at her waist. Her hair caught the morning light, making it look like a halo. "Obviously, you did what you were hired to do, and you did it exceptionally well. Is it always going to be David and Goliath cases?"

"Probably."

"Are you always going to be on Goliath's side?"

"I don't know. I hope not. What I really want is to

focus on my research. I know you know how fulfill-
ing that can be. It's such an amazing rush to follow the
trail of an idea, to discover something no one had connected." He sighed. "But in all the interviews, they keep
talking about me being in the courtroom. I don't hate
it there, but it's not me, you know? Especially because
the trial work would be in addition to the research, and
Christ, that just seems…difficult."

"So can't you just tell them what you want?"

His smile was crooked. "Not if I want to achieve my
goals. I mean, I really do want to step up. Forget it, I'm
just whining when I have no business doing any such
thing. I hit it lucky and big, and this is my moment.
That win is what's going to put me in the big leagues."

"No, I see that," she said. "But it must have been
hard, to have such a bittersweet victory at the root of
all this success."

He gently squeezed her leg. And didn't mention that
there hadn't been anything bittersweet about it. That
had come later. After he'd met her.

MAX HADN'T PLANNED on going to City Hall Park that
day. But when Joey Balaban had called, asking if he
had time to meet, he didn't even consider saying no.
He saw Joey right away at the fountain, standing with
his hands in his pockets, looking more like a student
than a criminal lawyer.

The park was crowded, as expected, but Joey spot-
ted him quickly and they headed off south, walking on
the well-kept lawn. "Thanks for coming."

"No problem," Max said. "It's good to get out, walk
around."

"I know I called out of the blue, but I was hoping I

could ask you a favor. About family matters, of course. The never-ending argument."

"I figured. What can I do?"

Joey shook his head and ducked to get out of the way of a running kid. "Next week, I'm setting up a meeting at Ivan's home. I'm going to tell them I want to talk about the lawsuit. I'll make sure Victor's clan is there, too. Nat and I have to sit them all down and tell them to knock it the hell off. The problem is, I might be a good enough attorney to represent them in court, but I'm easily dismissed as Luba's baby boy. And while they do respect Natalie, I don't know if the two of us will be sufficient to put this idea to bed permanently. I was hoping you'd come and help us make the point."

"That it's a foolish waste of money?"

"Yes, basically. And that they don't have any proof that anyone stole anything. They're just being stubborn old goats."

"They're not going to like that."

"Nope. But if you're there, and you tell them they'd be fined for wasting the court's time, I think they'll listen."

"They'll also hate me."

"I doubt it. Hanna likes you and Natalie respects you. Besides, they'll find something else to argue about soon enough. This war won't ever end. But at least it won't cost them both a fortune."

"Sure, I'll do what I can."

"Great. I'll set things up."

"No problem, but after next week, I'm back to work and I may not have the time."

"Okay. Thank you. Seriously, thanks." Joey paused in the shade of a cherry tree. "I also wanted to ask you about your firm. I've heard a lot of good things about

Latham, Kirkland and Jones, and I was thinking after my stint at Legal Aid, I might check them out."

"To be honest, I don't know that much about the criminal side of the firm. I do know they have an excellent reputation and the lawyers there are top-notch. I'd give them a try if I were you."

"Good to know." Joey nodded. "After this last case, a lot of firms have to be knocking on your door."

Max smiled, and shrugged, though he saw no reason to be closemouthed at this stage. "I'm seeing what's out there, testing the waters. I could very well end up staying with Latham. What other firms are you thinking about?"

They walked again, heading back along a different route. "I've got a considerable list, including small firms. In fact, that's appealing to me more and more. I'd like to work somewhere I could really get to know the clients. Work on cases that mean something to me."

Not surprised, Max just nodded. He imagined most Legal Aid attorneys were of that mind-set. "There are a lot of good reasons to go small, although being located in Manhattan is outrageously expensive, as I'm sure you know, which makes it difficult to turn down any case. But I can put you in touch with a couple of people in Brooklyn who might be able to steer you in that direction."

Joey's smile reminded Max of Ivan. "That'd be great. I've got some contacts from Harvard, too, so maybe I won't be cast adrift."

"Harvard, huh?" He took another look at the guy. "You've got to have more than your share of firms knocking at your door."

"Yeah." Joey gave a modest shrug. "Where did you go to law school?"

"Northwestern."

"That's a great school."

"It worked for me."

They were by the fountain again. Joey checked his watch, and then held out his hand. "I appreciate you meeting me here. At Legal Aid, we don't have the luxury of long lunches. Or any lunches, most days."

"It's got to be great working there, though, huh?"

"Yeah. I wish I could stay, but that's not the deal I made." He backed up a few paces. "I'll call you."

After Joey turned, Max didn't immediately head off in search of a cab. He walked north, not paying attention to much. Just thinking about what his father had said. Keeping his own promise to consider his next move carefully. He'd been so gung ho about the law growing up. He'd wanted to be Clarence Darrow, Thurgood Marshall, Abe Lincoln.

But then he'd grown up and seen the world change. To support a family these days cost a fortune. He and Mike had been lucky. Their uncle Roger had left them a nice bequest when he'd died in 1994. Enough to put them both through college, then law school for him and graduate school for Mike. With the rest of the money, his brother had opened his first gallery and Max had made the down payment on his loft. At the time, the market had been the lowest he'd ever seen it in New York. The monthly mortgage payment was still outrageous, but he'd always been careful with his finances.

He knew he wanted a family someday, later down the road, and he wanted to make sure they would always have enough, no matter what. He didn't have to save the world or even like his clients. But he did have to be smart about his future.

# 15

THE YACHT WAS owned by the senior partner of Daniels and Porter. Natalie recognized the name from their television commercials. According to Max, personal-injury cases comprised only a small part of the giant firm, which had offices in Los Angeles, Dallas, London, Paris and Dubai.

The cab dropped them off at Pier 56, where they were met by white-gloved attendants who were checking off names before escorting guests up the plank. "Is it called a plank?" she asked, leaning close to Max.

"I don't believe it is. I think it's a gangway."

"I like *plank* better. You never hear a pirate threaten to have his captor walk the *gangway*."

He grinned at her. "That makes me think of the Jets and the Sharks." He bent a little and snapped his fingers in an absolutely terrible impression of a gang member from *West Side Story*.

"You are adorable," she said. They moved up the receiving line. "How come you're so calm when this firm is so huge?"

He slipped his arm around her waist. "It helps that I'm with the most beautiful woman on the boat."

"Ah, so you're going to use outrageous flattery as your main tactic."

Max, who looked stunning in his gray suit, shook his head. "In this instance, they're going to be the ones using the flattery. I just need to keep my head and remember that it's all fun and games until you actually see the contract."

From the moment they'd stepped on the dock, he'd been checked out blatantly by women and men. It didn't hurt that the tie he'd chosen made his eyes shine a fascinating blue-green. She was decidedly not the most beautiful woman in sight, let alone on the ship. But she felt like the luckiest.

Truth be told, she was a bit intimidated by the number of lawyers all in one spot. And the unbelievably luxurious yacht. Thank goodness she'd had this dress. She'd spent a great deal on it two years ago for the Tribeca Film Festival, where Omnibus was a sponsor. With her recent upgrade in underwear, it fit her even better.

It was finally their turn to get on board, and Lord, what a sight. Subtly aglow with recessed lighting and artfully placed strings of white minibulbs, the very large open-deck area had roving white-jacketed servers offering food and several different cocktails, including Champagne. There was also a bar and a five-piece band playing the kind of jazz that you can't ever dislike out loud, lest you be thought plebian. Fitting, as most everyone around them looked as if they'd been selected by central casting. Thankfully, there were a few folks who seemed like real people. Like people she'd know.

Max grabbed them a couple of Champagne flutes as they made their first foray around the deck. Just as she was about to comment on the quality of the drink, Max was approached by a very distinguished-looking man. Bald except for a collar of short silver hair, the man stood ramrod-straight. She wondered if he was ex-military, or had just trained himself to look as intimidating as possible.

Max introduced Natalie as his friend to William Daniels, the senior partner and vice versa. Hearing Max call her that stung a bit, but then that's precisely what she was. No matter what she'd rather be. Daniels shook her hand and met her gaze for an appropriate amount of time, but as soon as he turned back to Max, she understood that things had gone from social to business. The conversation changed in tenor and topic, beginning with a compliment about Max's role in the tort case, and a question about how it had come about.

Max looked pleased, and as he told the story, she understood why. The FDA advisory wasn't, in fact, law. But Max's argument read that if a product was regulated by the federal government, consumers shouldn't be allowed to sue—and states had no right to pass regulations or issue health warnings more stringent than those given by the federal government.

Mr. Daniels approved. At least, that was her interpretation of the noise he made when the right side of his thin-lipped mouth twitched.

But the second Max broke eye contact with Daniels to look at her, she realized she needed to make herself scarce. The court had agreed with Max, but the outcome still bothered her, and she was there to support him. The last thing she needed was for someone to see her discomfort.

She slipped away, thinking she'd find out what food was being served. The hors d'oeuvres were bound to be exotic and fabulous and she wanted to try them all.

The first one she tried was a mini beef Wellington to die for and the second, an eggplant tartine. Then she heard a woman mention Max, and the hors d'oeuvres lost all their appeal. The way she said his name, first and last, was filthy. The woman was beautiful and her voice was positively salacious and a little drunk as she went on about how happy she'd be to show him the ins and outs of the office.

Natalie walked away, wishing she could do or say something terrifically witty that would shut the woman up, but she'd only embarrass herself, and worse, Max. Just knowing the kind of hours these people kept, she felt certain that it wasn't all business all the time at the office.

Max was still with the senior partner. Max's body language looked relaxed even though a few other people had joined them. She couldn't help hoping he wouldn't accept whatever deal they offered. Which was ridiculous. No matter where he worked, there would be gorgeous, powerful women who were far more like Max than she was.

She stepped aside for a couple to pass, and they looked so polished and aloof, she felt as if she'd sneaked onto the main deck from steerage.

It was as if she'd taken off blurred lenses. The glamour she'd been wowed by did a very good job of hiding the people underneath the facade. There was a similarity of style among the crowd. Chanel. Prada. D&G. Almost every heel she saw was five inches high, and she didn't see a single off-the-rack suit. The women were all lean, and while there appeared to be a little more leeway with the men, most were in good shape.

She had never felt so invisible.

Finally, she saw an older gentleman standing alone. His suit wasn't immaculately tailored and he looked as if he was guarding his full plate of hot appetizers. She approached him carefully, looking for signs she wasn't welcome, but when he caught sight of her, he smiled.

"Hello," she said. "I'm Natalie. I'm a guest of a guest, and he's busy talking shop. I hope I'm not intruding."

"No, welcome. I didn't expect to be talking to anyone during this party so, nice to meet you, Natalie. I'm Harry. Harry Ellerbach."

"Hi, Harry. What brings you here tonight?"

"I was invited. I'm the CFO of the firm. They always invite me, and these days I tend to show up."

"Why's that?"

"I lost my wife four years ago. We never liked parties much, so we used to stay home. But now? It's a big house, and I get bored of my own cooking. Whatever else you want to say about Daniels, he doesn't skimp on the food."

"What I tasted was delicious. How long have you been with D & P?"

"Thirty-two years."

"Wow. That's quite a long run."

He had a nice smile. Not the perfect white Chiclet teeth of almost every guest there, but an honest one. "It is. I keep things legal financially, and they put my kids and my grandkids through the best universities in the country. It's a good trade-off."

"So you like working there?"

"I wouldn't say I like it so much as I'm used to it." He held out his plate, but she shook her head at the offer. "I know where all the bodies are buried. Metaphorically, of course. They're like most big law firms nowadays. Billable hours are king, and people who aren't useful aren't kept. But that's the world, eh?"

"Yes, that's true."

"You're not a lawyer."

"How did you know?"

"Thirty-two years."

"Ah. No, I'm a film archivist at Omnibus. It's a—"

"I used to go there. With Annie. We saw a lot of great films there. We even took classes. I remember one was the Middle Ages in Film. That was excellent. Better than PBS."

"Thank you. That was due to our relationship with the film school at NYU. Have you thought about coming lately?"

He sighed. "No. But now that you mention it, that's not a bad idea. I think I'll get the schedule. I like those question-and-answer programs. The ones that make me feel as if my brain isn't turning to mush. There are only so many tax regulations a man can read."

She opened her clutch and took out one of her business cards. He didn't have a hand free, so she slipped it into his breast pocket. "Call me. Maybe I can give you a private tour before a screening."

He smiled, and then his face grew serious. "Who did you say you were here with?"

She looked behind her. Max wasn't with Daniels any longer. He was fully engaged with a half dozen younger people, one of whom was the horrible woman. Every eye was on him, and they all looked as if they were utterly captivated by whatever he was saying. "Max Dorset."

"Is that him? The good-looking one?"

She followed Harry's line of sight. "Yes."

"I assume he's considering joining the firm," he said, and she just smiled. "He could do worse. He certainly looks like he'd fit in well."

"He had a big triumph recently."

"Ah, yes. As I said. He could do worse. Or better. It

depends on how much of a scrapper he is. I don't know about you, though."

"What do you mean?"

"Well, believe me, this is certainly no criticism, but you seem very nice."

She wasn't sure what he meant by that. "And?"

He leaned closer and lowered his voice. "Very nice isn't seen as much of an advantage at D & P."

"Max and I are just friends, so I don't think I can hurt his chances."

"Oh, no, that isn't what I was implying." He sighed. "I shouldn't have opened my mouth. That's why I should stick to eating instead of talking."

"I would have been very sorry if you had."

"And the defense rests, Your Honor."

She laughed. "What?"

"You made my point." His smile was kind, yet sad somehow. He just looked at her, his expression torn, and she had a feeling he was about to say something she didn't want to hear. "Most of the people who make it at Daniels and Porter are constantly looking to accrue points. It's not enough for them to win. Someone else has to lose. You know what I'm talking about?"

"Yes." She swallowed, trying not to let on that he was getting to her. "I do."

"That attitude is encouraged. Nurtured. He'll do fine if that's where he gets his energy. A lot of people do."

They watched the crowd around Max. Some of the outliers left, only to be immediately replaced. But the attention was centered on him, and he was glowing. Obviously in his element.

He'd told her that he was just window-shopping, seeing what was out there. He'd also said he wanted to secure his future, which meant a big salary. But she'd never seen it all laid out like this. The way everyone was sizing him up. It wouldn't matter that his motivation was a solid career and financial security; there was no way any firm wouldn't want to exploit every facet of his abilities. And yes, he wanted the most challenging cases, but she doubted they'd let him stay in the background. Any firm would be crazy not to exploit his charisma.

The fight melted out of her. All the secret hopes that he would suddenly come to realize that he wanted a home life, that he wanted *her* more than another stunning win, were carried off on the wind of fabulous excess. She just wished she could see it as an opportunity for him instead of a dangerous web.

Either way, it wasn't her business. Except that she needed to give up any last romanticized thoughts she'd entertained about a friendship between them. He'd try, she had no doubt, but soon enough he'd have to cancel lunch plans. Nights together. Then the day would come when he'd stop calling altogether, firmly in his own orbit, in his own tribal world, with its in-jokes and status markers.

This party was a preview of things to come. She most definitely didn't belong on this boat. He'd barely looked at her since they'd come on deck. Turning back to Harry, she found he had cornered a waiter, one carrying absolutely beautiful cocktails.

"And what are those?" Harry asked.

The waiter smiled. "It's an exclusive cocktail called the Daniels Porter. Made with St-Germain, rum, lemon juice, local honey, absinthe and house-made blueberry jam."

Natalie laughed. "Jam?"

"It's very, very good, ma'am."

"How much of that is alcohol?"

"It's best if you're not driving tonight."

She lifted one off the silver platter. "Thank you."

The waiter bowed his head as if he'd been trained at Downton Abbey, and she sipped her drink.

"What do you think?" Harry asked.

"It's sinfully good."

"Of course it is. You should eat."

"Actually, I think I'm going to take a walk around the deck. I've never been on a yacht before and I don't want to miss anything."

"Would you like company, or is this a solo voyage?"

"Oh, yes. Please come. I'm sure you know more about boats than I do."

Harry put his almost empty plate on a nearby tray and together they set off to explore. "First thing you should know," he said, "is this isn't a boat. It's a megayacht. That's a whole new class. Basically, you could house an army here and keep them fed long enough to invade a small country."

"A megayacht. I'll remember that."

Harry walked slowly, which was fine. He led her toward the edge of the deck, naming things as he went. She knew exactly where Max was every step of the way. She watched the tide of guests wash in and out, while he was as steady as the shore. It was difficult, sharing him. It was hard not to think of their time together and how soon it would be over. She'd miss him. It. Them. He'd been smooth and interesting, and she'd never been as quick or as daring in her life.

She knew, absolutely, that he liked her. Without a doubt in her mind. They sparked, truly, but now she could see it was because they were flying above the real world.

This was where he belonged. He might like to see an old film now and then, but he'd found his métier in this old profession.

"You ready for another drink, Natalie?"

They'd reached the edge of the party area, where the white-as-froth decking met some kind of magical carpet that didn't seem to give a damn about salt water. The waiter with the Daniels Porter cocktails was waiting on her decision.

"You know, I think I do. One for the road."

"Already? You don't want to see any of the berths below?"

She looked unerringly at Max, who was laughing at something, looking like a prince surrounded by his people. "No, thank you," she said, her attention once again on Harry, who didn't seem to fit in at all, but obviously didn't give rat's ass. "I'll just make my way home. You, Harry, have been the highlight of my evening, and I hope very much to see you at Omnibus. We'll have a great time, I know it."

"Take care of yourself, Natalie," he said, the quiet compassion in his eyes nearly her undoing. "And take care of your friend. Make sure he doesn't get lost on his climb up the ladder."

# 16

DEEP IN A conversation about some of D & P's most unusual cases, Max was tapped on the shoulder. Even though the associates in his immediate circle had been far too nice to be sincere, he wasn't pleased at the interruption, especially when he saw it was a waiter delivering a note. Max didn't recognize the writing, but the message needed no signature.

> *Max, I wasn't feeling well, but I didn't want to interrupt your conversation. I'll be fine. No worries and good luck! TTYS, N.*

"When did she—?"

"She asked that I wait ten minutes."

He reached for his wallet as he scanned the crowd around him. "Thanks," he said, turning toward the prow. He knew she wasn't there, that there'd be no point, but he couldn't help it. It wasn't like her to slip away.

By the time Max had the twenty-dollar tip in his hand, the waiter had gone. Of course. Private party. No tip was expected. But he caught a glimpse of his watch and his heart flatlined for a second. How had time gone by that quickly? He'd left her alone for well over an hour. At one point he'd seen her speaking to an older man, but that had been awhile ago.

The man hadn't fit in with the extremely well-dressed crowd around him, and it was no surprise that Natalie had found someone who seemed out of place. Because she felt out of place. Jesus.

He looked again at his watch. He really had abandoned her. Left her to her own devices on a yacht where she knew exactly one person. Him. The schmuck who'd practically begged her to be his date.

There was a case to be made that she really wasn't feeling well. Even though the yacht was fairly stable, there was definite motion going on. She could have eaten something that disagreed with her, had one too many glasses of Champagne. But he wasn't buying it.

As nice as her note was, he could easily see her leaving because, frankly, he would have if he'd been in her shoes. However inadvertently, Max had basically tossed her aside. He tugged at the tie that felt more like a noose than was comfortable.

Dammit, she'd probably wanted to tell him to go jump in the Hudson, but she was far too nice to be so blatant when she knew this party was important to him. By now she was probably at home, cursing the day she'd met him and hoping for a freak hurricane.

He needed to talk to her. Apologize. Figure out if there was some way to make up for his appalling behavior. And, yes, find out if she was ill. Or just disappointed in him.

He glanced around. There had to be someplace private where he could make the call.

"Max?"

Turning toward the voice, he saw a guy he'd met earlier, a real Ivy League type. His name was Hamilton—

whether it was the first or last, Max couldn't remember. He motioned for Max to join the small group near the prow sipping cocktails. Max nodded, and gestured that he'd be along in a minute.

Before he could find a quiet corner, he was stopped by two equity partners who were having a friendly argument over how the FDA had responded to the tort case and wanted Max's thoughts. As urgent as it was to get in touch with Natalie, this was still part of his interview, and he didn't dare blow it off. He tried to be polite and not check his watch. When he finally did, he was stunned that another twenty minutes had lapsed. He should've just excused himself right off the bat.

A minute later he made the call, which went directly to voice mail. Natalie could still be in a cab, but he didn't think so. Or maybe she was talking to Fred. Complaining, no doubt.

He disconnected without leaving a message, waited thirty seconds while he cleared his head, and tried again.

She still didn't pick up.

He cleared his throat while waiting for the beep. "Hey, Natalie, I got your note." His mind went blank for a moment. "I'm sorry you're not feeling well." He paused again. "Look, I was a jerk. Time got away from me." He lowered his voice. "I was inexcusably rude. If you felt sick, I should have been there to help. I'm sorry. I need to talk to you. Call me. Please."

Of course, he had no idea what he was going to say to her if she did call. What he'd done was plain rude. God, she probably wasn't even going to call him back. But he double-checked that his phone was on vibrate before he shoved it in his pocket, One thing he did know, there was no point in sticking around. In fact, he'd be doing himself a favor by leaving. If he stayed, he'd undoubtedly put his foot somewhere it didn't belong.

So. Leaving. He had to handle himself well. No promises had been made, of course, but his conversation with William Daniels had gotten so personal, Max knew he would be getting an offer, and probably a damn good one.

He'd laid out the entire trail of his research on the seafood case. How he'd proceeded after his discovery. What his goals were both for the immediate future and beyond. This time, he didn't emphasize the business about wanting to be a researcher. If this experience had taught him anything, it was that he couldn't afford to be picky. Daniels hadn't sugarcoated the time commitment or the necessity of accruing lots of billable hours, and Max had kept his mouth shut about his pie-in-the-sky wish list.

None of what had transpired surprised him, except for the level of schmoozing from the other associates. Now that he wasn't in the midst of them, he could see that their spiel had been rehearsed. Not word for word, but the gist? They knew the game and played it well. Which made sense for an organization as large and successful as D & P. There had been a couple of uncomfortable remarks about his lack of an Ivy League diploma, but that wasn't unusual. The hierarchy of degrees was an unavoidable reality in his profession.

The whole thing had gone by in what felt to him like twenty minutes. He'd meant to bring Natalie back into the conversation, but he'd been swept up in the flattery like some rookie straight out of law school. It wasn't that he was being fawned over, although he was, but he'd bought into the inner-circle mentality of his contemporaries.

He'd compared this process to being rushed for a fraternity, and tonight had been a prime example. He'd acted like a freshman, and worse, he'd behaved like a child, self-obsessed and careless toward someone who mattered a great deal.

He'd wanted her to hear the words, see them competing for his attention. He'd wanted to impress her.

He found William Daniels in the salon, speaking to a beautiful blonde who might have been a model. Or at least someone he'd seen in the papers. Possibly his wife. Max waited until they'd finished up before he approached.

"Mr. Daniels, I'm going to have to leave sooner than I'd planned. My companion isn't feeling well."

Williams offered his hand. "I'm sorry you have to go, but the rest of the evening is just social. Now that you have some idea what the team is like, are you still interested?"

"Very much so. I certainly wouldn't be bored."

That tiny smile, the one that could have passed for a twitch, came back again. "I'm glad you stopped by. Someone will be in touch."

"Thank you. It was illuminating."

Williams walked down a hallway that must have led to the living quarters, while Max made his way on to the main deck. He couldn't help noticing the opulence in every detail, from the lamps to the carpets to the artwork. It was gorgeous, but he didn't think he'd actually want to hang out there.

The second he was off the yacht, he checked his phone to confirm he hadn't missed her call. He found a cab quickly, and after giving the driver Natalie's address, he pulled out his cell phone again.

There were no messages. Of course.

He'd try calling one more time, but when he got closer to her place. Maybe she'd still call him.

Tonight, more than any other time during his vacation, he'd felt the heat of ambition coursing through his veins. D & P was by far the front-runner of all the firms he'd talked with. Daniels and Porter was exactly what he'd had in mind when he'd hired Stella. He wanted the challenge, the kind of cases that would only go to a big and powerful firm. They were the group huge companies—hell, governments—turned to when they were looking for groundbreaking decisions that would tax him to the limit. The Supreme Court had seen William Daniels more than a few times already.

But Max would be signing his life over. He'd gotten spoiled in the last couple of weeks, having time to watch a game, eating out for pleasure, being with Natalie. He'd been so comfortable, he'd pulled his name from the dating-card group. The idea of not seeing Natalie for weeks, perhaps even months, at a time bothered him. And the notion of serial dating didn't appeal in the least.

Although all of that might be out of his hands, not by dint of hard work, but because of his own behavior. How could he blame her? She'd been so great. Dressing up in her beautiful purple dress. He'd been proud to be with her, until he'd become the man of the hour. He'd been certain they would have a great time after the wheeling and dealing were over. He'd even hoped that they'd have cause to celebrate.

But he hadn't thought it through. Not just the fact that he'd been swept away by all the talk of big cases and lots of excitement, but the fact that he'd brought Natalie at all. She'd told him once she was an introvert, and that big crowds were an issue for her. Then he'd left on her own.

Christ, he wanted to kick himself around the block.

It hadn't really hit him before, the disparity between Natalie's world and his own. She had the same kind of mellow energy as his folks, as Mike, at least when she wasn't talking about movies. He couldn't imagine what she must be thinking about the chest-thumping and pontificating she'd witnessed tonight.

He'd never claimed to be a prince, but he'd never behaved like such a selfish bastard before. His gaze went to his phone, and he thought of all the friends he'd lost in the last three years. Who was he kidding? He'd been a self-centered prick. He'd put his work before everything and expected everyone to pick up where they'd left off when he was ready.

"Buddy, everything okay back there?"

Max had no idea what the cabbie was talking about until he saw his hand, fisted against the window. He must have hit it, and now he could feel that he had, pretty hard. "Yeah, sorry. Everything's cool," he said, putting both hands in his lap.

He really had to hand it to Joey. The guy had a Harvard law degree. Max knew quite a few Harvard attorneys, and he'd met several more tonight. He'd bet his loft none of them had waited so much as five minutes to barter their degree for a fat salary and bright future with a top law firm. He would've done the same thing. In fact, he had. Northwestern graduates were welcomed, if not as actively recruited by stellar firms, and he'd capitalized on his class standing. It was the smart thing to do, so he had no problem with it.

But knowing Joey hadn't jumped at any of the lucrative offers Max was certain had been thrown at him was impressive. The guy had chosen a stint with Legal Aid while he weighed his options. Smart, very smart.

Max knew he'd get a lot of personal satisfaction working at someplace like Legal Aid. But he sure as hell wouldn't be able to furnish the loft, let alone set himself up with a nest egg he could rely on.

Being around Natalie and those good feelings she brought out in him had lulled him into thinking he might be able to have both, but he knew better. He'd been riding high after his victory. Exhausted at first, but feeling invincible. Somehow he'd forgotten that the last couple of weeks in no way represented the exhausting daily grind that had become his life. He could have the career he'd been counting on, or he could have a social life, but not both.

Natalie had been smart to leave tonight. She'd tried to steer them toward a friendship with that game of Scrabble the other night, but he'd pushed to add sex to the mix. By itself that wasn't a problem. For a lot of people. But not Natalie, and deep down he'd known that. He'd known that once the job took over his life again he wouldn't have the time to devote to a relationship. Still, he'd wanted what he wanted. The rules didn't apply to him. And why not? He was Max Dorset. Man of the hour.

Shit.

His hand was fisted again. He stretched it out, determined to quit all the histrionics. It wasn't like him. He hated this kind of melodrama. He'd been an ass. He was prepared to accept the consequences. Apologize for his actions and ask how he could make it up to her.

Three blocks from Attorney Street, he stared at his phone. If she didn't answer his calls, or never wanted to speak to him again, so be it. It would hurt, but he'd deal. But cutting him off wasn't like her.

He hit Speed Dial.

"Hi, Max."

"Natalie." Relief flowed through him. "Are you okay?"

"Fine. Better."

"Did I wake you?"

"No, I haven't been home very long." She sounded sleepy. Maybe she really wasn't well.

Or she'd been crying.

He took a deep breath. "I'm surprised you're speaking to me," he said and noticed the cab was now only a block from her building. Maybe he should've stopped for flowers. Maybe red carnations meant "I was a complete and utter asshole and I'm sorry" in flower language. "I got carried away, at your expense."

"It's fine, Max, really. I knew tonight was about work and I saw how they were treating you. I don't blame you at all. You were being courted. Anyway, neither of us could've predicted my headache." She paused. "So, are you impressed with Daniels and Porter?"

"They're definitely at the top of the list." Dammit, her voice was slightly off, but not by much. He couldn't get a read on her. "Tell you what...how about I come over and give you some old-fashioned—"

"No," she cut in just as the cabbie pulled in front of her house. "Stay at the party. This is important for you. I wouldn't be good company, anyway. I just need a decent night's sleep."

Max wanted to convince her to let him up, but for once, he listened to what she wanted. Which was to be alone. "Good. Okay. Get some sleep, plenty of fluids, maybe some aspirin," he said. "We'll talk tomorrow, huh?"

"Sure. Good night, Max. Have fun."

She disconnected before he could get in another word. Though what was there to say?

"Driver," he said, leaning forward. "Change of plans."

NATALIE HADN'T EXPECTED him to call. Not so soon. It had been tempting to let it go to voice mail, just as she had the first two times, but she didn't want him bungling his big opportunity because he was distracted by her. She wasn't angry and she didn't blame him, not really. But she was sad. Horribly sad. And disappointed, but mostly in herself.

Huddling in her ratty old robe, she slipped under the covers. But then she realized she hadn't turned off her cell phone and grabbed it off the nightstand. She didn't think he'd call back tonight. He was too busy being wined, dined and flattered. But just in case he did sneak in a call, she didn't want to choose whether to answer it or not.

Getting over Max was going to take awhile.

A lump formed in her throat and that was another perfect reason she shouldn't talk to him again tonight. Her emotions were simmering too close to the surface. Maybe if she gave in and let herself have a good cry she'd feel better. Though she had a feeling there would be plenty of time for tears ahead for her. She lay on her side and touched his pillow. Then tugged it closer to see if she could smell his scent. It was there. Very faint, though.

Maybe she was making that up, too.

She turned onto her back but that position left no room for fantasizing that she was curled up beside him. God help her, what part of disappointed in herself did she not get?

She'd told them they'd talk, and she meant it. She wasn't ready to write him off yet. At least he'd offered to come over, so that was something. He could've waited until the party was over, but he hadn't. And the truth was, he might've been a tool for ditching her, but he'd never promised her anything beyond friendship. He'd even warned her about how little time he'd have after returning to work. She remembered once being irritated with him for mentioning it…again. She'd had to stop herself from telling him *okay, enough, I get it already.*

Obviously she hadn't gotten it at all.

It was up to her to be very clear that they were only friends, casual friends who happened to have great sex. And that arrangement would last for as long as it lasted, and that was it. End of story.

## *17*

NATALIE SHOULDN'T HAVE been surprised when her phone rang early the next morning. Max knew she had to work. What he didn't know was that she'd be going in late. She doubted she'd gotten more than four hours' sleep and an event that evening would keep her at work longer than usual.

"Hi, Max. How did it go?" Her voice was as light and breezy as she could make it, but she doubted he was fooled.

"Glad to hear you're still speaking to me."

"Stop it. Of course I am."

"How are you feeling?"

"Better. Not a hundred percent, but better."

He hesitated. "Can you stay home and rest? Get someone to cover for you at Omnibus?"

"Nope. In fact I have to stay later than usual tonight. But honestly, I'm fine."

"Well, at least now I don't feel so bad. I'll be tied up, as well."

Natalie's heart sank. Which made no sense. What had she expected? For him to sit at home and mope every time she wasn't available? That he'd never go out again without her?

His free evenings were numbered. He'd be returning to work in a few days, and even if he wasn't busy with work, he'd still have his colleagues to meet and clients to talk to. Max would do whatever lawyers did after work, and he wouldn't think twice about it. The thought hurt, and that was exactly the kind of crap she had to stop. He owed her nothing. "You have another interview?" she asked, as if it meant nothing.

"No. Dinner with my folks. I promised them I'd go over before I went back to work. Mike and I are meeting up and taking the train to Bridgeport." Max sighed. "I almost forgot about it. Guess I'm an equal-opportunity jerk."

"Hey, come on."

"I'm so sorry," he said. "I'm still embarrassed about my behavior last night. Leaving you alone like that. Jesus."

Damn her traitorous body, but her eyes welled and closing them did little to help. "It's okay. I swear. I knew you'd be busy."

"And I knew you weren't comfortable in big social situations. But you were gracious enough to overlook my callous disregard and come anyway. I can't apologize enough."

"Thanks, but you have. Really. It wasn't all that bad. I met a very nice man, and we've even made plans to see each other again."

The silence on the line was satisfying, in a bad-seed kind of way. Which wasn't her style. "His name is Harry Ellerbach, and he's the CFO for the firm. He's only about sixty, but he lost his wife awhile ago. They used to come to Omnibus. He's lonely, and I think I can help him meet some people he'd like."

"You really had me going there, kiddo."

"Did I?"

He sighed. "Yeah. As if I've got any business being jealous."

That was the kind of stuff that would get her into trouble. He was right; he had no business being jealous. And she had no business being happy that he'd admitted it. "Look, I've got to get moving. I'm not ready for work yet."

"Right. I didn't mean to keep you. But any chance we can meet for lunch?"

She bit her lip. It felt awkward between them—too much hesitation and his voice sounded wrong. Had they already made it to the regret phase? Please, not yet. Maybe if they saw each other in person, things would be better between them. She knew she couldn't have him, but it didn't have to end cold turkey. "Possibly. I'll have to play it by ear. How about I call you?"

"Sure. If it works out, great. And if not, it's only an hour-and-fifteen-minute train ride to my folks' house. They aren't night owls, so I won't be back too late…."

His voice trailed off, letting the suggestion hang there. Until now he hadn't had any trouble asking her to spend the night at his place, or if he could stay at hers. In fact, words had rarely been necessary.

"We'll talk about that later, too," she said, her voice softening. "We sure got off track, didn't we?"

"I don't regret it," he said as if she needed convincing.

"I'm not certain what I feel."

"Oh, God, Natalie. Don't give up on us. There's no question we have a transition to make, and I'm not saying it'll be easy. But—"

"Max…"

"No matter what, I'm so glad I know you."

The resurgence of the lump in her throat was inconvenient. She'd tried her best to be steady and strong, even when her emotions were tying her into a knot. After swallowing several times, she managed to say, "I really do have to go. We'll connect later," before she hung up.

She dropped the phone on her bed and pulled her robe more tightly around her. Sadly, the sensation made her think of Max and how many times he'd come from behind and put his arms around her and cradled her against his chest. She was going to miss those things so much....

All her years spent studying film had given her a very well-defined understanding of the difference between a happy ending and a tragedy. There would be no delightful twist, no deus ex machina that would save the day. What she wanted and what Max wanted were miles apart. The accident of their meeting and hooking up was remarkable given their personalities and their goals, but it was unsustainable.

Of all the movie tropes she'd studied, the one she'd never connected with was the ill-fated love story. It was heresy, but in her opinion Ilsa never should have left Rick in *Casablanca*. Even though he'd acted like a condescending jerk, they would have been brilliant fighting the enemy together.

And the hell with *Titanic* and *The Way We Were* and *Brokeback Mountain*. All of those manipulative tearjerkers. Why fall in love when it could only end in heartbreak?

She should have said goodbye after their first night together. But it was too late to rewrite that script. The only approach she could take to get through this in one piece was to remind herself that she was a sensible person. Well, she had been before Max. But then, a lot of things had been different about her life before him.

Good thing she hadn't applied her makeup yet, because no amount of blinking could have stopped her tears. She just hoped she didn't look like absolute hell when she got to work.

LUNCH HADN'T PANNED OUT. Max couldn't say he was surprised. Disappointed, yes, but Natalie had sounded harried and there'd been a lot of background noise so he didn't think she'd blown him off. They were still tentatively on for tonight after he got back from his parents' house, so he was relieved that a plan was still in play. And frankly, while lunch with her would've shot to the top of his priority list, it would've required a lot of juggling.

Next week he had to go back to work, so he'd scheduled his last meeting for midmorning. It hadn't mattered that it was Saturday. The partners of Goldstone and Bridges were happy to speak with him, and he'd thought squeezing in a meeting with the small law firm would help make his decision clearer. The partners had been great. He liked Sarah and Marissa. Their reputation was stellar. They were on solid financial footing, had an excellent support staff and he'd been very impressed with their values, right down to how they chose their clients.

But they couldn't come close to matching the kind of offer he'd need to meet his most fundamental goals. He'd kind of figured that, but he was glad he'd explored the possibility.

Unfortunately, he'd left more confused than ever. On the one hand, he would love to spend his days with people who weren't driven by the bottom line. Not only were they not sharks, they weren't even trying to be.

Goldstone and Bridges was a concierge firm. They only represented people and companies they respected. What they needed at the moment was precisely a person with his skills and talents. He'd end up putting in the same hours and commitment, but for less than half the money, and the only promise was a yearly bonus of indeterminate size.

The issues Max had to consider had changed a great deal since…well, since Natalie. That first week off, he'd been barely conscious and hadn't been able to put two thoughts together. The second week had been squarely about maximizing his opportunity for a long-range win, knowing he'd face years of slavish work and that his sacrifice would be significant. But that was to be expected.

He was in this business for the long haul. Even if it meant putting some things on the back burner for now. That was the trick, wasn't it? Everyone he knew was putting off having a family and buying a house in the suburbs. Who could do all that and still hope to make partner by fifty?

So he'd do his best. Work hard now and reach his goals. Then he would find someone like Natalie and go the distance, wherever that led.

No, not *someone like Natalie*. It was crazy to think he'd be lucky enough to find anyone close.

He felt as if he were living in an O. Henry story. He'd found the woman he wanted to build a future with, but in order to have that future, he had to give her up.

He sighed as he realized he'd been walking blindly since he left the interview. It was already twelve-thirty, and he was supposed to meet Joey in half an hour. He'd meant to walk to the coffee shop near the Legal Aid office, but now there wasn't time.

Instead of a cab, he took the subway. As tempting as it was to keep rehashing his dilemma, he used the ride to read his email and check up on the news.

Joey had gotten them a small indoor table. With his venti americano, Max joined his friend. Well, not quite friend. What might have turned into a good friendship wouldn't ever get a chance to grow. "Having problems getting the family to cooperate with your plans?"

Joey shook his head. "Not really. Trying to decide on a date is the biggest issue. Lviv is closed on Mondays, so that's looking like the best day for everyone to come. Around two or three in the afternoon. Is there any chance that could work for you?"

"Actually, that sounds doable as long as it's in the late afternoon. I have an important meeting at ten-thirty."

"Terrific. Natalie will be there, which will help. Everyone looks up to her."

Max nodded, wondering why she hadn't mentioned it to him. It was ridiculous to feel as if he were the one being edged out of her life. Especially given what had happened last night. But this sit-down that Joey was arranging was the type of thing she would've talked to him about.

"That's not the only reason I wanted to meet." Joey studied his coffee for a minute before meeting Max's eyes. "I think I've decided what I'm going to do after I'm finished with Legal Aid."

"Oh?"

"It's radical. But the more I think about it, the more I like it."

"You've got my attention." Max drank some coffee, barely noticing he'd forgot to put in his sugar. Thankfully, there were a few packets on the table, so he grabbed one.

"I'm going to start my own firm."

Max stopped tearing the packet open. "Really? Your own firm?"

"Yep. I know I need experience, and that's why I'm going to need a partner. Someone who has a track record, and could give the firm the kind of credentials we'll need to make a real go of it."

"And, I'm assuming, a hell of a bankroll?"

Joey looked down at his hands. "Actually, money isn't the problem."

"Oh." Max wasn't sure what to say. He hoped Joey had done his homework and given this decision serious thought. Understanding that he needed a partner with experience since he had so little wasn't enough. It made more sense for him to use his Harvard degree to put a high-profile firm on his résumé than have to ride a partner's coattails. "Where are you thinking? Manhattan?"

"Yeah. Maybe Brooklyn. Probably Brooklyn. I've got money. I've invested well. I could work for someone else, learn the ropes in a more traditional way, but honestly, that's not my thing. Working at Legal Aid has been enlightening. Combined with my two years being an intern at Goulston & Storrs, I know that I'll do better with my own team, without having to worry about fitting in at an established practice."

"That's a huge undertaking," Max said.

Joey grinned. "I know. That's what's got me excited. I like a challenge. I mean, I thrive on that kind of thing. To start with, though, I need to be damn sure about who I want to partner with. Or to be more accurate, who'd want to partner with me. You wouldn't be interested, would you?"

Max made a point not to laugh. "It sounds exciting," he said, and it was the honest truth. "But I can't see that happening. Sorry. I've just reached the sweet spot, you know? Where I'm being sought after. I think I'd enjoy working with you, but man, you're talking about a hell of a risk."

"Not with the right people. I'm not going to jump into something until all the pieces are together. Fortunately, I've got the means to do that. There are a few other people on my short list. I'm not just looking for one super attorney, but to create a team. I've already put a lot of effort into the business plan with the help of my financial advisor. Anyway…" He finished off his coffee in two gulps and checked his watch. "I've got to head back to the office."

"Go ahead. I think I'll get something to eat while I'm here."

Joey got to his feet. "I wish I had more time. I've been wanting to pick your brain about what you've gone through. Maybe I can buy you a meal or something, when I don't have to run off so fast."

"I'd like that," Max said.

"Great. I'll give you a call about the time for Monday's meeting," Joey said, backing away. "If something comes up and you can't make it, let me know."

"I'll be there." Part of Max wanted to tell him to forget about the whole business. No one did that, fresh out of school. It was crazy and reckless and he'd probably lose all his money, and those were only the first things that came to mind.

The other part of him was jealous as hell. The audaciousness of the plan alone had Max rubbing his hands together. To dare something so outrageous was damned impressive. He'd be in charge of clients. Of structuring the firm to suit the team's talents. Knowing what he did about Joey, Max figured he'd be too busy to breathe for the next year or so. But in the end, Joey could do a lot of good for a lot of people. He was clearly smart as hell, and if he could build enough equity to put a plan like his together, imagine what he could do to build his firm? Damn. If Max were a betting man, he'd back the kid.

What a family Natalie had. Hell, half of them were bat-shit crazy, but they sure weren't people you could ignore. Bigger than life. The kind of characters books were written about.

No wonder Natalie loved movies so much. Look who she'd grown up with. Look who she'd turned out to be.

He thought about their first night together. How brave she'd been. Scared to death, but willing to seize the moment. She'd been thrilling. He'd never thought of a woman in that way before, but it fit her. She was a whole different kind of courageous.

Whatever else happened, he was going to keep Natalie in his life. Someway, somehow. It didn't matter what form it took as long as the thread between them didn't break. That was doable, no matter what offer he accepted.

And tonight with any luck, he'd be with her.

Between now and six, when he had to be at the train station, he was going to make a list of all the things he wasn't willing to negotiate. Then he'd start going down the list of firms. Carefully. Thoughtfully. Like he'd promised.

On Sunday, he'd still be at it. Giving himself the time to look at every angle. His meeting with the senior partners at Latham was scheduled for Monday at ten-thirty. They would make him an offer, and the ball would be in his court. There would be no room for a mistake.

# 18

LAST NIGHT HADN'T worked out.

Natalie had been equally sad and glad. No, that was a lie. She'd been sad and scared.

Max's dinner with his family had gone late, and by the time he'd reached Penn Station, she'd been in bed, exhausted from having had too little sleep and being strung out emotionally. Who knew what she would have done if he'd showed up in person.

At least she'd gotten more sleep than expected. Probably because her body wanted nothing more to do with her thoughts. Work had been a blessing, because she'd had two great tour groups and had caught their enthusiasm while she'd been with them. The moments in between, when her defenses were down, the roller coaster was right there, midswoop.

They'd made plans for Max to come over, and now that his arrival was imminent, she questioned her sanity. Twice she'd almost called to cancel, but this was it for them. Their last night together.

She'd see him on Monday at Lviv, but that marked the official beginning of their friendship. Tonight was the end of their affair, their swan song, and like an addict, she had to have one more hit.

Her reflection in the mirror confirmed that her anguish was written all over her face. She'd try to pretend it was simply the result of insomnia and working too much, but Max was no dummy.

So she'd planned an evening that would take the most pressure off. The idea of talking about their situation tied her stomach in knots, so she had a Blu-ray disc in the player. *Roman Holiday.* Befitting and encouraging. Even Audrey Hepburn didn't always get to keep the love of her life.

Oh, God. She couldn't think of Max like that. She couldn't be that masochistic.

He was due any minute. She'd ordered a pizza to be delivered soon, as well. Maybe at the same time. The bed trays were all set up, the remote was on her bedside table. The beer was still in the fridge. Everything was in place.

Including a full box of tissues within easy reach of her bed, because who was she kidding?

She paced around the house, stopping at the appropriate windows to look for him on the street, and paused in her bedroom. She'd thought about wearing only her kimono to greet him, but nixed that idea quickly. Now she was beginning to doubt what she had gone with.

It seemed utterly ridiculous to have put on her La Perla underwear underneath a simple shift. She peeked down the scoop neckline and decided her boobs looked as good as they ever had. No. This had been the right choice. Not to turn Max on, but to make her remember that she was brave, and that she could do this and even if she blubbered like a fool, she could still walk away proud.

The doorbell made her jump. Adrenaline screamed through her veins as she flew down the stairs. It was Max.

He pulled her straight into his arms, right there on

the threshold, and kissed her as if he needed her more than air, more than anything.

She let herself sink into him. Her thoughts scattered into a million bits, but each one was about Max. His taste, the way he smelled, the fact that she would know him from the touch of his hand on her back, or the shape of his ear.

A circumspect cough behind him pulled them apart, and Max paid the red-faced delivery kid before they went upstairs.

There was no undressing as they got on the bed, no more breathtaking kisses. But his fingers brushed hers when he took his plate. A smile that was so bittersweet it made it hard to swallow.

"It's not as if I'm going off to war or anything," he said as they settled in place for their viewing party.

"Right," she said, borrowing his light tone. "We'll still be in walking distance."

"I've figured out that we're sort of equidistant from Katz's. So, I see a lot of early-morning bagels in our future."

"Exactly," she said, putting on an easy smile that went south halfway through. She ate a whole veggie slice and missed almost everything that happened on the screen. Another piece was out of the question when he offered.

Their eyes remained locked, though, after she shook her head. A moment later, the pizza box landed on the floor, as did both the stupid trays, and she clung to him with her hands and her legs and her kisses.

Hours later, she quivered through a full-body orgasm as he thrust into her so deeply she felt marked, and together, they came apart.

No description could have captured the moment more precisely.

HE WAS DRESSED and ready to go at six-thirty. She was still in the bathroom, still in her robe and putting on the finishing touches of her makeup. Thank God he didn't have to be at Latham for a few hours, because *shit*.

When she walked into the kitchen, she had her favorite mug in hand and tried to hide the small tremor, but he caught it. As if she could fool him now.

He might not be shaking, but there was no doubt he was shaken up. Just last night they'd been in her bed, his body and hers connected, and not just through kisses and sex. It was hard to believe he had no idea when that would happen again. Or if it should.

He put his empty mug down. He wanted to kiss her properly, but that wasn't a good idea. Instead, he pulled her close and rested his forehead against hers. They shared the same mint-and-coffee breath as they stood there. He wished he could exit on a witty line, something reassuring and hopeful. Instead, he said, "You're amazing. I should have said that every day. And I'll see you this afternoon."

She sighed, her fingers clutching the bottom of his jacket. "You're amazing, too. Go out there and grab your moment and the future you've always dreamed of."

He pulled back. "I feel like we should make a date for next week or something."

She just smiled that lovely smile. "Probably best if we wait and see how things roll out."

Max nodded, knowing she was right even though he didn't like it. Before he could do something stupid, he left.

The morning air was chilly, but he didn't even consider catching a cab. He needed the walk. There was so much to think about. It was tempting to linger on Natalie, on the astonishing two plus weeks they'd been together. If felt as if it had been months instead of weeks until this moment. Now he resented every second he'd missed being with her.

Although seeing his folks and Mike had been a good thing, he couldn't deny that he'd missed her. It would have been great if Natalie had come with him, but then again, maybe not. He'd needed the time with his family. Especially watching his parents, married for thirty-two years and still enjoying each other's company more than anyone else's.

He might never wake up to her again. That thought had bugged him on the train, had risen several times last night, and each time it had come out of nowhere and bothered him terribly. They hadn't had enough time, that's all. Two weeks was nothing. There were too many things he needed to learn about her. Everything from her favorite ice-cream flavor to what she thought of the designated hitter.

But he did know that she made him think. In the immediate aftermath of the tort ruling he'd just wallowed in the victory, along with all the other people in his world. It was a cause for celebration. But after he'd met Natalie, he realized that while he was proud of the victory, he wasn't so proud of the outcome.

It honestly made him wonder what had happened on his way to becoming a hero. He knew that answer. He'd become driven and egotistical. He'd lost friends, deservedly. And he'd forgotten some important lessons.

All the while, he'd been with the bravest, strongest woman he'd ever known. Even though she'd wanted to get married, she'd refused to settle. She'd gone after what was important, not what was easy. Hell, why on earth would she settle for him, after how he'd behaved?

To think he hadn't immediately called his family

when he'd finished with the case was mind-boggling. That he'd avoided Natalie's questions was more than telling. Not that she'd let him get away with his obfuscation. She'd asked him all the right questions.

But was he asking them of himself? His father had told him to look at all the options. He hadn't, though. He'd gone through his offers, the firms, the choices that would lead to his dream future. But that picture was pretty damn narrow. Where did his folks fit in? His friends? Natalie?

He'd been so busy thinking about where he'd want to end up when it was all said and done that he'd forgotten to consider who he wanted to be when he got there.

He slowed his step and stopped, blocks past his loft. But that was okay, because his mind was as clear as it had ever been. He was ready for his meeting, and he knew exactly what he was going to say.

THE KNOCK AT HER DOOR panicked Natalie a little. Had Max forgotten something? She dabbed at her eyes and quickly checked her reflection before seeing that it was Fred outside. Of course. Max would have rung the doorbell downstairs.

"You okay?" he asked the moment she opened the door. "I just saw Max leave."

"Other than the fact that it's over between us, I'm swell."

"What do you mean it's over? What happened?"

She shook her head and looked at her watch. She'd gotten dressed too early, and now she had time before she had to be at work. "Nothing unexpected. I mean, I'll see him later at Lviv to help Joey squash the lawsuit nonsense."

Fred followed her into the kitchen as she started to make some more coffee. She'd need it.

"Okay, so it's not *over* over."

"It is. I mean, we both knew this was coming. Tomorrow he goes back to work, and then, well…you know."

She heard Fred shift behind her. As much as she wanted him there, she didn't want to start crying again. But dammit, listening to her whine about her pitiful life was what Fred was for. Putting down the coffee tin, she turned to face him. "I screwed up. I kept telling myself it was temporary and I could handle it."

"I know," he said, sliding in beside her to take over coffee-making duty.

"Max is at the peak of his career, has amazing skills with a solid plan for his future. He's got motive and opportunity to see his dreams come true. So why in the hell would he put all that aside for me?"

Fred snorted, but didn't comment.

She watched him set the grinder at the wrong grit and didn't care. "But I'll give him credit. He never once lied to me. I knew right from the start who he was and what he wanted out of life. I walked into this with my eyes wide-open, so no matter what, I can't blame him."

"Sure you can. Make it his fault. I always do, whether I'm wrong or right. Eventually, you'll have to take responsibility for your part, but in the meantime, screw it, blame him."

She mustered a smile. "Too late. I'm already at the taking-responsibility part."

"Then how about the part where it's no one's fault?" He looked at her, his eyes full of pity. "You two clicked. No one can predict when that kind of alchemy will strike. On paper, you guys should have been oil and water. But that's not what happened. Truth is, you both got lucky."

She waved at her face, at her puffy eyes. "Lucky?"

"Yeah. There is no way in hell you're going to end up with some schlemiel now. You've had Oliver and you've had Max, and sweetie, there is no way you're going back to the minors."

"You're right. So I'll just go down to the perfect-men department at Macy's, shall I? I'm sure they have a wide variety, and I'll customize him to fit my exacting specifications."

"Look, you've got that whole trading-card thing going on. Seriously, you've got a great path to follow now, better than most. And you'll just have to do what everyone in this city does—say yes to every damn date you can."

"The whole point of the trading cards is to separate the chaff from the wheat. And anyway, that won't help me forget Max."

"You can't know until you try."

Natalie didn't say anything. She knew he was trying to help, but he didn't understand. Max was the most amazing man she'd ever met. Someone whose path she should never have crossed. Yes, he had flaws. She was still bothered about his big victory, not just about how many people had been hurt by the verdict, but that Max had known it was ethically questionable or he'd have told her about it their first night together. And after watching and listening to people on the yacht Friday night, he seemed headed right back into those murky waters. The thing was, though, he wasn't built for being that kind of shark. He could be as tough as nails, but to be true to who he was, he needed to be on the white-hat side of things. She'd thought long and hard about that and she wasn't wrong.

"What happened to you two staying friends?"

She leaned against the counter. "If he goes back into the same environment, despite his best intentions, he'll be buried."

"Not necessarily."

"And I thought I was the unrealistic one living in movie land."

"Hey, I like Max. But I love you," Fred said, getting a smile from her. "I'd be the last person to push you at him if I thought he wasn't good enough for you. He's pretty and I assumed that's what had turned your head. Game night proved me wrong."

"The story about his brother in the hospital?" she asked, sighing with the memory.

"Cool as that was, no, that's not it. It was really obvious that he wasn't into game night, even after he won. The part he liked best was being with you."

She hadn't really thought about it, but Fred had a point.

"And yeah, the hospital story about his brother and father?" Fred pretended to swoon, making her smile again. "Jesus. Killer. That's the kind of stuff that builds character from the ground up."

She nodded, thinking about him as a little boy in his Superman suit. "See, that's the thing… I know that side of Max. That is so him. His dad is still his hero. I think Max might want to be a hero himself. But Friday night on that yacht—you should've seen it with the over-the-top Champagne and all the women who were collectively a size two—it was as if we'd stepped onto a movie set, except I was horribly miscast. That's when

I really got it, how different we are from each other. We live in different worlds that should never overlap."

"Oh, sweetie...." Fred sighed and then frowned. "You know what? This coffee looks all wrong. I think I screwed up."

"You did."

"Huh," he said, giving her a look she didn't understand. "So people really can change," he said, very unsubtly.

She swallowed hard. Fred was trying to help, but he'd only reinforced what she'd discovered for herself. On that yacht, Max had showed exactly how he'd changed. The little boy in the hero costume was gone. At least on the outside, but she knew the good man was still there. Would it still be if he accepted the job at D & P? "I know that Max has it in him to be a remarkable man. The man I've fallen in love with. But he won't if he keeps reaching for security instead of satisfaction and honor."

"So what are you doing to do about it?"

Natalie blinked as she recalled the words of Harry Ellerbach. How he'd counseled her to take care of herself and her friend. And Max was her friend, at least for now. She owed him the truth. He probably wouldn't be delighted to hear what she had to say, not right before he was supposed to begin work again, but she couldn't stand by and not tell him the truth.

So she would. Today. After the family meeting, she'd talk to him. Face-to-face, friend to friend... The whole truth and nothing but the truth. Which would probably take care of the shaky friendship issue.

Damn, but she really, really hated irony.

NATALIE WAS TRYING her hardest to pay attention to Joey, who was standing in front of five tables of family and laying down the law. It was a hell of a talk. So good that even Ivan and Victor had shut up to listen. But she kept looking at Max, sitting to her right, at the same table.

The two of them had done their parts, small as they'd been. She'd told them that if they wanted either restaurant to succeed, they had to start behaving like real chefs instead of children. That had gone over big, but her point was made: enough of the yelling. People came out to eat to enjoy themselves, not to listen to soap-opera screaming.

Max had spelled out what a nuisance suit could cost them. As the figures climbed, the two men had shrunk in their seats, finally hearing how ridiculous all the fighting had become.

But Joey was actually offering them a compromise, something they could both be proud of. Each of them could make a new signature dish. Not the same kind of dish, but something they could call their own. It would reflect the Ukraine and their heritage, but have a new American twist. They could publicize the unveilings together, and have customers coming to both restaurants. Then they could find something else to argue about—but not at the workplace.

It was brilliant and simple, and Joey truly did look like a big-shot attorney. Max had been smiling for a while, at least every time she'd caught him staring at her.

"Everybody clear?" Joey asked. There were grumbled mutters but no one raised an objection, so Joey raised his voice to say, "Okay. Everybody out. Now."

Victor started to protest, but Joey cut him off. "Max and Natalie need some privacy. So, everyone, go."

Ivan stood up and opened his mouth, but Luba, Hanna and three other cousins herded him into the kitchen.

Natalie turned her chair to face Max. "I asked him to do that. I hope you don't mind. I need to talk to you."

He shook his head. "Since I asked him the same thing, I think we're fine. You want me to go first?"

She shook her head no and took a deep breath. Putting it off wouldn't make it easier. "No, I do. I'll go first."

Max looked behind her, and she turned to find Aunt Hanna sneaking up to the table, holding a white candle.

"I'm a ghost, not even here. Just let me light this and I'll vanish." She took a match from the book, but before she struck it, Natalie winced and held up a hand. "No, Aunt Hanna. Thank you, but no. We don't need a candle."

Hanna frowned, but she went to take it back.

"Wait," Max said. "It's very nice of you. Please, I'd like the candle lit."

Natalie felt a little sick. He wouldn't be so happy about the bit of romance when she got finished with her speech. He probably thought the candle would make her feel better about everything, about them being friends, but how would he feel when she told him he should quit the job he'd just accepted?

The candle fluttered, then held the flame, and Hanna made a quiet exit.

"Go ahead," he said, a small smile playing at his lips. She'd soon take care of that.

"I'm not sure what firm you decided to go with, but I think it was probably Daniels and Porter. And as your friend, I need to tell you that, well…" She sat up straighter and clasped her hands together. "I think it's a mistake. I'm sorry, I should have spoken up before now, but I couldn't live with myself if I didn't at least try. You're too good for them, Max. They're not nice people. And please don't laugh. I know lawyers aren't renowned for their kindness and courtesy, but they were really terrible people. I wasn't even around them very much, and I knew that.

"The thing is you're not like that. You're a really good man, with strong values and a big heart, but if you go there, and bury yourself in that environment, I'm afraid you'll lose the best parts of yourself. I know you want challenging cases, but maybe there's still a way to find that while fighting for things you believe in."

She took a deep breath, barely able to look into his eyes for fear of what she'd see. But when she pulled her courage together and met his gaze full-on, his eyes were as warm as the candle they reflected. "Did you hear what I said?"

He nodded. "Oh, yeah. Is it my turn now?"

She could only blink, but she thought she'd gotten the message across.

"I agree with you completely."

That made her blink some more.

"For a couple of days now, I've been going over my options. I've looked at a very long list of pros and cons, and weighed them as straightforwardly as I was capable. One of my top picks had almost everything I wanted, but one of the senior partners was an ass to a waiter and his driver, and that turned out to be a deal breaker.

"In fact, that whole win-at-all-costs attitude wasn't fitting so well. But instead of just crossing all those firms off the list, I decided to throw the list away and start again. Except this time, instead of putting all my energy into my future life, I thought, what if my life starts now? What would be on my list, if I could have my ideal situation right this minute?"

He leaned over and put his hands on hers. "And that's

where you came in. Because it's really hard for me to see a lot of satisfaction in a life that doesn't have room for you. I don't mind working hard, but I don't want to be swallowed whole. You saw the truth about D & P, and honestly, that's not the way to what I really want. That's a one-way ticket to a heart attack at fifty.

"So I decided I'm going to stick with Latham for a couple of years, but under my terms. No more killer hours unless it's absolutely unavoidable. A hefty bonus and more say about what cases I work. Also, less time in the courtroom."

It took her a minute to find her voice again, because she was reeling with all this astonishing information. He'd obviously thought things through. Which meant... "Really? They'll really do that?"

"For a couple of years," he said. "Then it'll be re-negotiation time, but that's okay. That'll just make it easier for me to move over to Joey's firm. Kid's got a hell of a head on his shoulders. And he's pretty family friendly. Which is good, because I want kids, and not when I'm too old to enjoy them."

"But wait." She pulled her hands away, because she couldn't touch him and say what she needed to. "I'm not the right woman for you. You need someone out-going and sophisticated who buys designer dresses. I didn't tell you this to manipulate you into liking me, I was being a friend. For real."

His crooked smile helped her to settle the butterflies in her stomach. "Telling me what you did proves you're exactly the woman I need. With you at my side, I might just become the man my father hoped I would be. The man I want to be for my kids.

"You gave me the courage to rethink my options. Hell, you didn't settle for Oliver, and you walked boldly into situations that scared the crap out of you and you never blinked. A woman like you is hard to come by, and I don't want to miss out on what we could build together. So what do you think? Would you consider joining me on this wild ride?"

She stared at him, letting it sink in. It wasn't easy. And she knew the road ahead of them wouldn't be, either. But she couldn't imagine going any other way.

"Say yes, you foolish child," Hanna said, her voice carrying from the kitchen.

Both Natalie and Max turned to see the family nearly tumbling out from the swinging door. Of course they'd been eavesdropping.

"You can still change your mind," she said. "I come with all those lunatics."

He stood, pulling her up with him, and his kiss told her a lot, but not as much as his whispered, "Are you kidding? You're the total package. I couldn't ask for more."

\* \* \* \* \*

# REQUEST YOUR FREE BOOKS!
## 2 FREE NOVELS PLUS 2 FREE GIFTS!

### red-hot reads!